Copyright Notice

ISBN: 978-1-953668-08-0

Author's Note

It was all supposed to end with 'Trapped', but due to high demand, the story *had* to continue. Everyone who enjoyed Trapped continued to ask me how the story continued; I can proudly say that I believe you will all be amazed at how the story turns out.

"Trapped" was released on August 25, 2016. Anyone who truly knows me knows the irony of the release date, but here we are exactly one year later with the sequel. I wrote 'No Turning Back' with methods to jerk at your emotions; it will make you laugh, parts of it will make you angry, and parts of it will make you cry (from both sadness and happiness).

'Trapped' *was* the story, 'No Turning Back' is the result of that story being told. Be sure to let me know what you think and leave those reviews!

Be *YOU-tiful* and remember not to let anyone tell you the sky's the limit, when there are footprints on the moon.

Dedication

I truly want to say thank you for supporting me in this journey. I greatly appreciate your love and support, as it is what motivates me. So many things inspired me to write this piece, including the thought of releasing another work to satisfy you all, my fans. I would like to take a moment out to thank my family and friends for their consistent words of motivation, as those also play as factors that keep me moving forward.

As you read this new piece, I ask that you read it, as though you've never known who B.M. Gage is; as though you've never heard my voice before; as though you've never listened to my show and have NO IDEA how I think. Read it with a new mind; if you don't know who I am, that's even better! All I ask is that you learn more about me by listening to my show on WWMR-DB: The Heat, https://theheatdb.com, and following my Facebook page (facebook.com/officialbmgage) and my twitter (twitter.com/officialbmgage).

1

"Isaias, it's going to be okay," Kaiden tried to stay strong and comfort the child. But in reality, he knew things would be difficult.

Kaiden looked over and saw Sandra and Gary; both of them were extremely emotional and had eyes full of tears.

Kaiden continued to scan the room and saw two men he didn't recognize sitting in the front row; a few people down from Sandra and Gary. Kaiden wished to ask who they were, but he knew it wasn't the time nor the place for such questions.

Kaiden couldn't help but notice the daisies that were placed meticulously around the church. The flowers seemed to be in full bloom.

Aside from the flowers, he also noticed many balloons and gifts brought by family and friends. Yet, he *only* saw Christina's family and friends... none of his were there.

Christina wore a white dress with ruffles across the bottom.

Her hair was so neatly done, that Kaiden couldn't help but put a hand in it.

Kaiden let out a few silent tears. He had a feeling this day would come, but he didn't expect it to come so suddenly.

He laid a kiss on Christina's cheek. As his lips left her face, he felt as if he could feel her soul latch onto him.

"Baby, I love you," Kaiden whispered. "You can finally rest," he silently cried. "Isaias is safe with me, I promise."

Kaiden knew that if Christina had to choose anyone to raise Isaias, it wouldn't be Jordan, it wouldn't be Trequan, it would be him.

Kaiden didn't want to brag, but he possessed such a positive influence on Isaias' life, that he knew he would raise him right.

Kaiden walked away from the casket while holding Isaias' hand.

Isaias cried harder because the container was so high that he couldn't see his mother.

Isaias wasn't old enough to understand death, but from everyone else crying, he knew it couldn't have been anything to be happy about.

But Kaiden didn't want Isaias to see his mother like that; he didn't want that to be the last image of Christina that Isaias had in his mind.

As Kaiden walked away from the casket, the ushers closed it.

He took a seat next to Sandra and Gary, to show that he was still family to them, no matter what he and Christina had been through. Truth be told, regardless of all the heartache that Christina had put him through, she would *always* have a special place in his heart. She was his first true love and even after the breakup, he would continue to think about the plans they'd discussed, the love they made, and the silly things they would do.

The organist concluded the song that she was playing, and the church inhabitants seemed to silence in unison.

The choir director motioned his hands downwards, and the choir took their seats.

"We are all gathered here today," the pastor began, "to celebrate the life of Christina Parker."

Sandra couldn't control her emotions.

"My baby!" she cried out.

Kaiden reached out his arms and pulled Sandra back down.

"Why'd He have to take my baby?" Sandra cried as Kaiden hugged her. She cried into his arms and as she cried, Kaiden let out tears and rubbed her arm.

He kissed her on the cheek as she cried harder.

"A life taken too soon, ladies and gentlemen. We have got to do better," the pastor continued. "Christina was a beautiful young lady, inside and out," the pastor looked at the crowd. "I look into the crowd and see all of these faces: family, friends, coworkers; Christina was loved by many."

He cleared his throat and looked at Sandra.

"I know this must be a difficult time for the family. Mrs. Sandra Parker-Johnson, my sincerest condolences to you and your husband. I know how hard this must be for you right now."

He directed his focus back to the audience.

"But I want for you to know, that whenever you're feeling down, you have this whole crowd of people here today because they love you and support you," the pastor spoke as the members of the church applauded.

"Although Christina's spirit has left her meat vehicle that was used to get around on this Earth, her spirit lives on."

The audience continued to applaud.

"She's always at your side," the pastor paused and received louder applause and praise from the churchgoers.

"She's in the building right now. Blessing us all," the pastor finished and the audience abrupted in cheers, cries, and applause.

As the applause subsided, he spoke again.

"Now, you all are used to me giving a sermon, but the beautiful Christina has approached me many times before and told me that I should try to switch it up and that I needed to get with the times."

There were scattered chuckles at the pastor's joke.

"So, since we are celebrating her life, I'm going to let you all speak on a special moment you may have shared with Christina."

Kaiden tapped Sandra and she sat up. Gary put his arms around Sandra and Isaias, while Kaiden walked to the microphone.

"Good morning, ladies and gentlemen," Kaiden began. He looked back at Christina's closed casket. He walked back towards the casket and touched it.

Kaiden still couldn't believe that Christina was dead. He raised the microphone and continued to speak.

"My name is Kaiden Green, and I'm going to be honest," he inhaled sharply. "Christina was my first love." He swallowed air and continued to attempt to speak, but the words wouldn't come out.

Kaiden was so startled at the thought of Christina dying that he awoke from his sleep. Tears fell from his eyes.

Jada felt him jerk and woke out of her sleep.

"Baby, what's wrong?" she asked him.

Kaiden took a deep breath but didn't speak. Jada put her hand on his bare chest.

"You had that dream again, huh?" she asked.

Jada was a little annoyed that Kaiden still had dreams of his ex on some occasions, and she could tell this dream was about death, but she didn't let it bother her much.

She couldn't. She had her own secrets and skeletons to deal with.

Kaiden didn't respond in any form. Because of this, Jada kissed his cheek.

She didn't know how to comfort Kaiden. She knew that he knew it was just a dream, but she didn't want to offend him by saying 'it was just a dream', which would ultimately be telling him to suck it up.

To comfort Kaiden, she rubbed his chest.

"It will be okay," she finally spoke.

Kaiden shook his head as he felt a tear form in his eye.

Even after everything that occurred with Christina, he still had plenty of love for her and felt strongly about such ideas.

"You just don't know," he mumbled under his breath as he laid back down.

Jada laid her head on his arm and put a hand on his chest.

Jada kept her head tucked low to prevent Kaiden from seeing the secrets and worry in her eyes.

Kaiden was so disturbed by the dream that he didn't wish to go back to sleep.

He closed his eyes and hugged Jada tightly.

The warmth of her body against his was just what he needed to feel, but he still felt empty inside.

Jada tightened Kaiden's grip around her waist and cuddled closer to him.

"Kaiden, give me a kiss," Jada spoke.

Kaiden looked at Jada. She was absolutely beautiful to him.

In the amount of time that Kaiden had moved into his own house, Jada visited quite frequently.

Kaiden had a 4 bedroom, 2-bathroom home with three floors.

Jada thought this was too big of a home for one person, but Kaiden needed a place to store all his equipment since he wasn't a fan of storing data online.

The master bedroom was where Kaiden slept at night. In room number two, Kaiden had a server configured so that when he did his recording and production, he could save all his work 'online' but locally to his own private and secure cloud. Room three was his guest room, where people would sleep if they stayed the night and room four is where he stored his extra equipment in case he ever needed to set up additional microphones, condensers, filters, etc.

The rooms were all upstairs, which were all safeguarded with codes except for the guest room. One the first floor is where one of the bathrooms resided. The kitchen and master computer resided on the first floor, in addition to his sitting room and additional storage closet, and in his basement, was where he set-up his in-home studio, complete with the soundproof room, the mixer, microphones; the complete package.

He kissed Jada and held her tightly.

"I don't want to let go," he whispered in her ear.

Jada was silent for moments before she spoke.

"I'm not going anywhere," she assured him.

Jada and Kaiden had been dating for two years. But in those two years, he often found himself thinking of Christina and the things they'd been through: the experiences they shared, the memories that remained in his mind, the love they made.

"I love you," he spoke to Jada.

His words were sincere and true. Kaiden loved Jada and would do whatever he had to do to prove it to her. He'd opened his heart and now that she'd entered, he feared the worst at times.

"I love you too," Jada replied. "Let's get some rest."

■■■

Christina woke up and cuddled with the bear that Kaiden had gotten her during their relationship.

A 36-inch brown bear with a heart rested in her arms as she scrolled through her phone.

She couldn't continue to punish herself over what happened with Kaiden. It was the past, and as far as she was concerned, what's done was done.

Isaias ran into her room holding her iPad.

"Mommy!" he spoke excitedly as he held the device to her.

She looked at the screen and saw an image of her, Isaias, and Kaiden holding hands.

"Mommy, look at Daddy," Isaias excitedly spoke.

Christina's eyes immediately began to water as she saw the picture of the three of them. Part of her was happy that Isaias had this memory of Kaiden after two years, and part of her was sad that even after she'd tried to make things work with Jordan and explained to Isaias that Jordan was his father, he still referred to Kaiden as 'Daddy'.

"Baby, no," she answered. "That's Kaiden, not Daddy," she replied as she wiped her eyes.

Although she and Kaiden ended their relationship two years ago, she, like Kaiden, found herself thinking about the times they shared.

She knew that she would never find anyone like Kaiden, no matter how hard she searched. She'd found people to crave her sexual appetite, comfort her when she was feeling lonely, and people to hang out with, yet, even while she was doing things with other men, Kaiden remained on her mind.

He'd proved to her that he wanted Christina for her. Kaiden made her feel good consistently, not just for the moment.

"Isaias, is it bad that I'm trying to find Kaiden in everyone I date?" she asked although she knew he wouldn't answer the question.

Christina picked up her phone as Isaias walked off with the iPad. She decided she would give Samantha a call.

Christina was glad that even after Kaiden and Samantha had a fling, she and Samantha were able to remain friends. However, the two didn't communicate nearly as frequently as they did before the breakup.

Christina dialed Samantha's phone number and held the phone up to her ear. She truly wished to call Kaiden, but she chose not to do so.

"Hello?" Samantha answered.

"Hey, Sam," Christina spoke. "How are you?"

Samantha was surprised to hear Christina's voice on the other end of the phone.

"I'm good, girl," she excitedly spoke, "how about you?"

"I'm doing well," Christina partially lied; she told alternative facts or fake news, as the generation would say.

"Oh, that's good," Samantha spoke as she combed her hair. "How's Isaias and moms doing?"

Kaiden had such an influence on her life, that even though she was talking to Samantha, she could hear Kaiden's traits and way of speaking. When she heard Samantha say 'moms', Christina knew Samantha got that from Kaiden.

"Everyone's well over here. I got up a few minutes ago and figured I'd give you a call."

"You got plans for today?" Samantha asked her.

"Nah, me and Isaias have no plans." Christina sat up and looked at her doorway so she could see Isaias sitting on the couch. "Not a single one."

"You all know the zoo has free entry for the next month," Samantha suggested, "how about we take the little man down there? You know he loves the lions."

Christina chuckled.

Isaias *did* enjoy going to the zoo and mimicking the different animals he saw, especially the lions.

"Yeah, that sounds cool," she spoke. "When are you going?"

"I'll be heading out in the next two hours. I could come by and pick you all up, if you'd like," Samantha responded.

"Well, let me get my ass up and get dressed," Christina laughed. "I'll see you in a bit, girl," she said to Samantha.

"No doubt," Samantha chuckled as she hung up.

Christina got out of the bed and walked into her sitting room. Isaias sat on the couch watching television, as he typically did in the mornings.

"Wanna go see the lions?" Christina asked.

Isaias squealed with excitement.

"Let's go, Mommy," he stood up and walked towards the door.

"We gotta get dressed first," Christina laughed. "Gotta give you a bath because you are a stinky little boy," she joked with him as she pulled him close and began tickling him.

"Mommy," Isaias spoke with laughter, "stop!"

"Come on," Christina replied with a chuckle as she stopped tickling him. "I'll race you to the shower," she finished as Isaias ran to the washroom.

Christina walked into the washroom and turned on the water. She ensured that it wasn't too hot or too cold for Isaias and proceeded to give him a shower.

Once Christina showered Isaias and she took one, she emerged from the washroom with a towel on her head.

"Baby, go get dressed," she told him

She traditionally allowed him to pick out his clothes. To only be going on five years old, Isaias was quite the designer and was pretty good and choosing what to wear.

Christina applied lotion to her body and put on some jeans and a fitted pink t-shirt.

Christina walked into the kitchen and made a few sandwiches for herself, Samantha, and Isaias. She also packed chips and drinks so that they wouldn't have to pay for food at the zoo.

She left the kitchen once she finished the food and went into the living room.

She put multiple items in a bookbag, including a camera, sunglasses, sunscreen, and other items they may have needed or wanted for the trip.

Samantha texted Christina's phone and alerted her that she was outside, and Isaias walked into the room.

"You ready?" Christina asked him.

"Ready," Isaias responded cheerfully.

Christina picked up the bag and Isaias walked out of the door.

She followed behind him and closed it, ensuring it was locked.

Isaias was thrilled to see Samantha's truck as he walked up to the door and opened it.

"Hey, guy," Samantha chuckled as he opened the door. "You ready to see the lions?"

"Yes!" Isaias excitedly exclaimed. "Let's go," he spoke while simultaneously closing his door.

"We gotta wait for your mama to get in the car," Samantha chuckled as Christina opened her door.

She and Christina embraced as Christina closed her door.

"Damn, you're getting old, Christina," Samantha laughed as she reversed from the parking lot.

"Yeah, well if I'm getting old, what does that make you?" Christina chuckled.

"Better," Samantha instantly replied.

"You are crazy," Christina uttered. "What's going on with you?"

"Not much. Been working like crazy," Samantha spoke. "I'm glad I got a day off."

"Consider yourself lucky," Christina chuckled as she looked at Isaias through the rearview mirror. "I may have inherited money, but being a mother is a full-time job in itself. But I wouldn't trade it for the world."

Christina snapped her fingers and got Isaias to look at the mirror. She blew him a kiss and he blew one back.

"Who's mommy's best friend?" she asked.

"Auntie Samantha," Isaias responded.

Samantha and Christina couldn't help but laugh at his reply.

"Okay, who's mommy's other best friend," Christina spoke as their laughter subsided.

"Mommy has a lot of friends," Isaias started. "She's got me, Auntie Sam, Sabrina and her husband, Tory, and Daddy."

Samantha looked at Christina with a puzzled look. She thought that after the stunt that Jordan had pulled months earlier, Christina wasn't speaking to him.

"Daddy?" Samantha asked aloud.

"Yeah," Isaias replied.

"Who's Daddy?" Samantha asked as Christina also displayed signs of curiosity.

"You know Daddy," he began.

Several seconds passed by before Isaias spoke again.

"Kaiden," Isaias finished as he continued to play with his toy dinosaur.

2

Samantha drove into the zoo's parking lot and looked over at Christina, who'd fallen asleep. Isaias was in the backseat, anxiously looking out of the window for the sight of any animals.

"Ready to go see these lions?" she asked him.

Samantha was still a little stunned by the fact that Isaias referred to Kaiden as his father. She knew Christina introduced Isaias to Jordan and told him that Jordan was his father, but in Isaias' mind, it made more sense to consider Kaiden as his father.

"Yes!" he spoke as he tugged on the door handle.

"Slow down, cowboy," she joked. "We gotta wake your sleepy mama," Samantha tapped Christina on the shoulder.

Christina slowly opened her eyes as she looked around.

"Good morning, sleepyhead," Samantha chuckled as she turned off the car.

"We're here already?" she asked.

"Well, you did sleep the entire ride," Samantha laughed as she grabbed her wallet from the center console.

"You all set, Isaias?" Christina asked him as she looked in the backseat.

"Come on, Mommy," he spoke. "It's time to go see the lions," he fidgeted with the door handle once again.

Christina chuckled and opened her door before opening Isaias'.

Isaias quickly unbuckled his seatbelt and got out of the vehicle.

"Mommy, listen," Isaias tugged at his mother's sleeve as he heard an elephant trumpet.

"I hear it," Christina answered. "Do you know what that is?" she asked.

"An elephant," Isaias replied almost instantly as he held his dinosaur.

"That's right, big boy," Christina replied.

Samantha emerged from the back of the vehicle wearing sunglasses.

"Yall ready?" she asked.

"Yes, mam," Christina answered.

"Let's go," Isaias eagerly spoke as he took the lead.

"IDs, IDs, you need your IDs to see the monkeys for free," the security officer spoke.

He looked down at Isaias, who was still holding his dinosaur.

"Sorry, little man," he chuckled. "We don't have any more dinosaurs here."

"I want to see the lions," Isaias spoke.

The security officer chuckled.

"Well, I think you're in luck. We have plenty of those for you to see. Where's your mom? Does she have her identification?"

Samantha and Christina caught up to Isaias and the security officer.

"Mommy, the man needs your i.. i... *identitication*," he struggled to say the word.

Christina and Samantha both chuckled.

"How are you doing today?" Christina asked the security guard as she pulled out her license.

"I'm pretty well, how about yourself?"

"I'm good, thank you."

Samantha pulled out her license and handed it to the security guard.

"And how about yourself?" he asked Samantha.

"I'm well. Ready to relax," she chuckled.

"Well, I'm glad that you ladies are doing okay today. And what's your name?" he asked Isaias.

"Isaias," Isaias replied.

"Isaias," the security officer replied. "And how old are you?"

"5," he spoke as Christina held his hand.

"You're a big boy, huh?" the officer spoke. "We got a new exhibit that I think you'll enjoy," he started.

"And what's that?" Christina asked.

The officer stood up and spoke directly to Christina.

"Since Isaias enjoys the lions, I think he would enjoy the idea of being caged into a car that rides around and allows the animals to roam free, climb on top of the car, and live in their natural habitat."

"So we'll be inside of a car and the lions will be walking around us?" Samantha asked. "Sounds a little odd," she chuckled.

"We're trying it out," the officer replied. "Animals don't deserve to be caged in, so in reality, the environments that the animals live in here at the zoo, that's not normal."

Samantha looked at Christina.

"They come out when they feel like it, but we've developed a course, with trained drivers, that drives a caged car through the zoo, right beside the animals. We allow them to roam free and live how they're supposed to," the officer finished.

"That sounds like it could be fun, yet scary," Christina chuckled. "Thanks."

"You all have fun," he finished as he returned the licenses to the ladies.

Christina and Samantha walked into the zoo with Isaias happily leading the way.

"Ari, we have to have this down," Kaiden spoke from the other end of the recording studio. "Come on, girl, sing it like we discussed. Dig deep."

Kaiden press play on the mixer and the instrumental began to play over the speakers.

Ari gave Kaiden a thumbs up and closed her eyes.

"Why do you, why do you, why do you, why do you-ou-ou?" she began to vocalize.

"Yes!" Kaiden whispered.

"I give my love, my heart, my soul. Baby boy just take control," she continued to provide vocals over the background singing.

Kaiden's favorite moment was when he was in the studio recording. He felt as if a good number of his worries disappeared.

He pulled out his phone and noticed he had 4 missed called from Jada, he also saw a text from her.

Jada: Where are u??

Kaiden rolled his eyes at her text. This wasn't the first time that Jada acted like this. Often times, Kaiden wondered if the relationship was worth it. Times like this made him remember a line J. Cole put into one of his songs: *"the bitch wants too much, hits my phone too much, if I gotta be frank about it"*.

Kaiden: I'm in the studio laying down tracks.

Jada immediately replied.

Jada: y u ignore my calls?

Kaiden didn't reply. Jada knew that when he was in the studio, there was a good chance that he didn't hear his phone ringing.

"So, tell me why. Why, oh why, oh why. My heart hurts! The pain is in my soul," Ari began to get emotional during the breakdown of the song.

Ari kept her eyes closed as she sang soulfully.

"I love you, yes I do. But I can't take this from you, no more," Ari finished as the track ended.

"Beautiful," Kaiden spoke over the microphone. "Come on out here."

Ari excitedly removed her headphones and placed them on the stool, and emerged from the recording room.

"Let me hear that," she spoke as she stood next to Kaiden.

"You went into a place that I didn't even know existed in Ari Love."

"You told me to dig deep," she chuckled. "I just had to take it back to a recent heartbreak," Ari shyly admitted.

Kaiden pressed play on the computer and played the recording.

"Well, whatever it was, it worked," he smiled.

As Ari listened to the track, Kaiden could see her glow. Music was Ari's passion, and to be able to do it with someone who made her feel like family as opposed to an employee, was amazing to her.

Although Kaiden served as her manager, he treated her, as well as all of his artists, special, but there was a bond with Ari that he developed. He could see that she had the potential to go far, and he wanted to help her go the distance.

As the track ended, Ari jumped up and down with giddy.

"Great session, right?" Kaiden asked.

"You did the damn thing, Kai," Ari clapped her hands.

The two of them embraced when Kaiden heard a pound on his front door.

He saved the song on his system.

"Let's go see who this is at the door," he spoke as they left the studio and went upstairs.

Kaiden looked through the window and saw Jada frantically banging on the door.

Kaiden sighed as he opened the door.

"Why the hell aren't you answering your phone?" Jada asked as she walked inside.

Kaiden cleared his throat and Jada turned around. She saw Ari.

Ari waved a few fingers at Jada.

"What is *she* doing here?" Jada asked.

"Well, before you just came and caused a scene, we were downstairs making some new hits," Kaiden spoke calmly.

"That's what they call it now?" Jada eyed him up and down. "Drop your pants and let me smell your —."

"Yup, that's my queue to go," Ari spoke.

She didn't like controversy, especially when it wasn't necessary, and Ari knew this was going to become a situation.

Ari grabbed her coat from the couch and Kaiden helped her put it on.

"I'm sorry, Ari," Kaiden began. "I'll call you," he told her before she walked out of the door.

"Let me know," she spoke as he watched her walk to the car.

Ari drove away and Kaiden closed the door.

"The fuck is wrong with you?" he asked Jada as he walked downstairs to the studio.

"What's wrong with me?" she asked. "I'm not the one ignoring calls from my girlfriend and all this other shit," she followed him downstairs.

Once Jada reached the bottom step, Kaiden pressed play on the mixer and played a song over the speakers.

Jada was silent for moments before Kaiden continued.

"See, this is what the hell is wrong."

"So this is what you all were recording?" Jada tried to change the subject.

"Are you done acting crazy and insecure?" Kaiden shook his head.

"I'm sorry, Kai," Jada walked closer to him and put her arms around his neck.

"How many times are you going to say you're sorry before you actually stop?" Kaiden asked as he moved her arms from around his neck.

Jada didn't have an answer.

She leaned in to kiss Kaiden and connected her lips with his.

Kaiden didn't want to fight with her, so he allowed her to kiss him and didn't fight back.

"Do you forgive me?" she asked as she retreated from the kiss.

Kaiden looked at Jada.

Her hair was in a ponytail and she wore a fashionable outfit, complete with 4-inch heels.

"I can't say I do," he finally answered. "But I'll take another kiss and consider it," Kaiden gave in.

"You drive me crazy," Jada spoke as she put her arms back around his neck and kissed him.

"Nah, baby girl, you were born crazy," Kaiden corrected her with a chuckle.

Jada rolled her eyes as Kaiden stopped the track.

"Come on," he spoke as he locked the studio door and they walked upstairs. "Let's go out."

"You're not gonna try to kill me for acting crazy, right?" Jada joked.

"I just may," Kaiden laughed. "I'm hungry," he spoke. "You want to grab a bite to eat?"

"Like what?" Jada asked.

"I'm down for anything," Kaiden answered. "It's about 3 and I haven't eaten yet."

"Whatever you want," Jada spoke as they left the house.

"Mommy, look," Isaias spoke to Christina as they sat in the caged car.

He observed a lion crawling on top of the car, as another lion walked close to the car and put his nose next to the cage.

"I see it, baby," Christina spoke as she held Isaias tightly. "Let's try to get Auntie Sam to pet him," she chuckled.

"You're funny," Samantha laughed. "I'm not crazy, now."

"One thing I've learned about these lions," the driver spoke as he heard the two talking, "is that as long as you're patient and calm with them, they're gentle. Why do you think you have to be trained to drive on this course?" the driver laughed. "I start speeding, we'll have lions chasing us."

"And we do not want that," Christina laughed as she held Isaias' hand.

"Mommy, I want to touch him," Isaias tried to pull away from her.

The driver put the car in park and rose from the chair.

"If he wants to pet the lion, I could walk him closer. I'll show him the proper way to do so," he offered.

"I don't trust anyone with my baby," Christina protected Isaias.

The driver walked over to the cage and petted the lion's back, and once the lion turned around and put his nose to the cage, he petted the animal's nose.

"As I said, as long as you're gentle with them, they'll be gentle with you."

"Please, mommy," Isaias pleaded.

Christina kissed him on the forehead.

"You better guard my baby with your life," Christina spoke to the driver with a chuckle.

"Come on, little man," the driver motioned for Isaias to come closer.

Isaias held out his hand and walked to the driver.

Although he was excited, he was also nervous. He'd never been that close to a lion before, although he enjoyed watching them.

"Okay, now open your hand all the way," the driver spoke.

Isaias opened his hand all the way.

"Okay, now turn your palm over," the driver spoke and Isaias followed directions. "Slowly stick your hand outside," the driver instructed as Isaias stuck his hand out of the cage.

The lion looked at Isaias' hand and sniffed it. The lion licked the child's hand and Isaias shrieked and jerked his hand back.

The lion ran off, frightened at Isaias' sudden movement.

Christina jumped up.

"It's okay," the driver clarified. "But don't pull your hand back like that," he spoke. "He's okay," he assured Christina.

He slowly inched Isaias' hand back to the cage and a new lion approached and sniffed the hand.

"Try not to move," the driver whispered as the lion licked the child's hand.

The lion gave Isaias four licks before the driver spoke again.

"Slowly turn your hand over and pet his nose."

Isaias hesitated but turned his hand over and rubbed the feline's nose.

Christina couldn't believe what she was seeing. She pulled out her phone and began to record Isaias.

The lion moved and adjusted so that Isaias could rub his back.

"Are you seeing this?" she whispered to Samantha.

"I see it," Samantha spoke, "but whether I believe it or not is a different story."

Samantha and Christina were amazed at the sight, and Christina shed a tear.

She'd never seen Isaias happier than he was at this moment.

"Isaias, turn around," Christina called to him as he slightly turned his head.

He smiled and spoke.

"Look, mommy, it's a lion," he was smiling from ear to ear.

"Watch this," the driver said as he pulled Isaias' hand back into the car.

Isaias ran over to his mother, all smiles.

Christina kissed Isaias and Samantha did the same.

"You were such a big boy," Samantha spoke.

The driver spoke a foreign language and all of the lions seemed to give him their attention; including the ones on top of the cage. He threw a piece of meat out of the cage into the field.

In an instant, all of the lions roared and began to run for the treat. The lions on top of the cage jumped off and rushed to the treat as well.

Christina and Samantha both applauded as the driver walked back to his seat.

He said another term in the language and all of the lions stopped attacking the meat and looked at the cage. In unison, they let out a roar as the driver began to slowly drive away.

"And I got all of this on video," Christina was excited.

She knew that this was a trip that Isaias would never forget.

She stopped the recording and uploaded the video to her Facebook page with the caption, 'my big boy and the lions'.

Samantha opened the app on her phone and shared the video with her friends, and returned the phone to her purse.

"Bye, lions," Isaias called out.

Christina gave him another kiss on the cheek as the driver continued on the path.

"I can't believe that just happened," Samantha told her excitedly.

"My baby boy got to pet a lion."

Isaias was truly in disbelief.

The driver returned to the start of the exhibit and opened the door. He assisted the three out of the vehicle and they walked onto the pavement.

Christina reached in her purse and pulled out a five-dollar bill and handed it to the man.

"Thank you for making my little boy so happy," she smiled.

"As long as I can make children smile and happy, I know I'm in the right line of work," he responded as he declined the money. "His joy is more than enough of a payment."

The driver turned back around to the other parents and children who'd lined up to take a ride through the exhibit.

Isaias sat down at the table, and Christina knew that meant that he was hungry.

She and Samantha walked over to the table and sat down.

"What'd you bring?" Samantha chuckled.

"Sandwiches. Just like they make in prison," Christina laughed.

"And you would know this, how?" Samantha began. "You've never been in the joint."

"Shit, but when you got a baby daddy that's been in and out, you learn a thing or two."

Christina gave Isaias his sandwich, a Capri Sun, and a bag of chips.

"Speaking of baby daddies," Samantha spoke as she grabbed a bag of chips, "have you heard from that scrub?"

"No you didn't just call him a scrub," Christina laughed as she took a sip of her water.

"I call it as I see it," Samantha laughed. "He ain't shit, he never was shit, and he's ain't ever gonna be shit," she opened one of the water bottles after eating a chip.

"You're so stupid," Christina joked. "But no, I haven't heard from him. I don't really think I want to hear from him."

"What about Kaiden?" Samantha asked as she sipped the water.

Christina paused as the memories rushed through her mind.

"I mean, we say 'hey' every now and again, but nothing too extravagant," Christina spoke. "Why'd you ask that?"

"Because," Samantha showed Christina her phone, "he's got a charity event coming up in Chicago."

Christina studied the flyer on Samantha's phone.

"It's three months away," Christina responded. "What are we gonna do with Isaias?"

"Take him with us," Samantha ate another chip. "I'm positive that he wants to see Kaiden." Samantha unwrapped the sandwich.

"You think that's a good idea?" Christina asked.

"It's worth it. We all need a vacation and this could be the getaway. You get to see Kaiden again and see what he's up to."

"Girl, I'm not even thinking about Kaiden," Christina lied. "Shit, and I know he isn't thinking about me. We both agreed it was for the best that we didn't try anymore. It just kills me that Isaias is still calling him daddy, although he knows that's not his father," she whispered.

"You're going to see Daddy?" Isaias heard them talking about Kaiden.

"See what I mean?" Christina chuckled. "Yes baby, we're thinking of taking a trip to go see *Kaiden*."

"When?" Isaias asked.

"In a few months," Samantha replied. "If mama stops playing," Samantha tossed a chip at her.

"You know what?" Christina stated before throwing a chip at Samantha.

The two of them laughed as Isaias continued to eat his sandwich and chips.

"You wanna go see Kaiden, Isaias?" Samantha asked.

"Yes," Isaias began, "I like Kaiden. He's fun."

"He is," Samantha replied as she remembered the bond that Kaiden and Isaias shared.

"We still have time to decide," Christina took a bite of her sandwich.

***

Hours later, the two ladies and Isaias got back in the car to return home.

Isaias was asleep, so Christina unfastened his seatbelt and carried him.

"Thanks, Sam, it was nice hanging out with you today. We gotta do it again really soon," Christina spoke through Samantha's car window.

"We will," Samantha replied. "I'm gonna text you when I get home."

"Okay. Let me go put this heavy little boy down," Christina chuckled as she walked to the door and unlocked it.

She gave Samantha a final wave before walking inside her home.

She lied Isaias down in his bed before removing his shoes, pants, and shirt. She walked into her room and changed into her pajamas before entering the sitting room.

She pulled out her phone and went to her Facebook application.

Kaiden hadn't been mentioned in forever and the fact that Samantha brought him up had Christina curious as to how he was doing and what, or who, he was doing.

Christina typed Kaiden's name into the search bar and went to his page. His personal page was still private, so Christina couldn't see much or do much snooping. His celebrity page wasn't private, but he only used that page for promotion and to connect with his fans.

"Failed attempt," she chuckled aloud.

She put her phone away and turned on the television; to her surprise, he was on the news speaking about his upcoming charity event.

"Kaiden, although this is a local event, you've decided to promote it on a national network. Why is that?" the news anchor asked.

"Sharon, I'm glad you asked that. All my life, I've been a local guy. You know, throwing small house parties and listening events at these mom and pop shops. But it's time for me to branch out and expand my horizons. Even the largest concert I've thrown was promoted locally and through social media, but if I target a larger scope and do it through a different outlet, I can better spread my message," Kaiden kept his head held high as he spoke to the reporter.

Christina smiled as she saw Kaiden speak.

"Yeah, keep feeding them what they want to hear," Christina spoke aloud and mimicked him, although she knew Kaiden wasn't one to put on a mask for the camera.

Christina rose to her feet and walked to the kitchen.

She looked in the refrigerator and pulled a wine cooler out. She opened the top and returned to her place on the couch.

"Well, Kaiden, thank you so much for taking the time out of your schedule to talk to us. You know you're always welcomed here," Sarah finished.

"It's great to be here, thank's for having me," Kaiden finished as the channel faded to a commercial.

Christina's phone vibrated and she saw it was a text from Samantha. She unlocked her device and read the message.

Samantha: I'm home

Christina replied without thought. She was glad that her friend made it home safely.

Christina: Good! Stay there lol
Samantha: there's something wrong with you haha
Christina: Kaiden was just on tv
Samantha: word? For what? What'd he do this time lol

Christina rolled her eyes.

Christina: shut up lol. He was talking about his upcoming event.
Samantha: ahhh, so have you given thought about going? Lol
Christina: not yet lmao. I'll think about it.
Samantha: Well, the clock is ticking lol. Don't ponder it too long
Christina: Yea, whatever lol. Goodnight
Samantha: See you tomorrow. I'll come through and hang with you and the little guy

Christina: Sounds great

Christina locked her phone and walked into her room. She put her phone on the charger and got into her bed.

She pulled her bear close to her and closed her eyes.

3

Kaiden finalized the track that he and Ari worked on weeks prior. He'd given her a call a few hours earlier and asked for her to come by.

Kaiden heard a buzz at the door and rolled his chair over to the monitor that rested on the wall of the studio. He pressed a button on the control panel and saw Ari standing at the front door, and he pressed a button to speak over the intercom.

"Ari, I'm in the studio, I'm coming up now." He released the button and walked up the stairs and opened the door for her.

"Welcome back," he chuckled as she walked into the home.

"Are we alone?" she joked as she looked around.

"Just me and you. Maybe we can get some work done today," he hugged her. "You on the dating scene yet?" Kaiden asked her.

"Now you know I'm on the market, but not really," she chuckled.

"Yeah, well let these guys know about me," he laughed. "You're like a sister to me and you know I'll be the first to be on the scene if a guy acts up with you."

"I know," she laughed. "Feels good to know that someone genuinely has my back and doesn't want anything in return."

"Oh, but I do," Kaiden answered.

Ari's smile vanished from her face.

"Your friendship and talent," Kaiden finished. "That's it."

"Well, you got that," her smile returned.

"Come on," Kaiden spoke. "Let's go finish up before Jada *attempts* to destroy what we're making."

Kaiden led the way downstairs before speaking.

"I've mixed it down, put all of the background vocals where they should be, woo wop da bam," Kaiden laughed.

Kaiden pressed play on his system and the song played for Ari to hear.

"I hope you did me justice," she spoke as the song started.

Kaiden didn't reply. Instead, he smiled at her as the song began.

Ari knew that once the vocals began during the review, a word was not to be said.

Kaiden pulled out his phone and checked his email as he waited for the song to end. A text from Jada came through, but he didn't bother to check it.

His focus was on his work, and if Jada couldn't respect that, Kaiden had no use for her.

"I'm loving it," Ari spoke excitedly as the song ended. "I like how you put some of my vocals in the background as if I were speaking down a long hallway."

"Yeah, I wanted to capture that effect as if you were calling out to the guy as if he were walking away from you. But there's no way I can take all the credit for this," he chuckled, "it's all you. No need for autotune or anything when I work with you."

"That's how you know it's real," Ari chuckled. "This is that hit for radio. Let's send this out, like yesterday."

"If only we could," Kaiden replied. "Gotta get it registered and everything else. That is if you want to get paid from it," Kaiden laughed. "You wanna get paid, right?"

"That's the overall gameplan," Ari shrugged.

"If it gets your seal of approval, we'll send it off now. Or, we could wait and build a buzz. Get your cover art circulating, continue to work to develop your album; you know, the smaller things that will mean a ton when the moment comes."

"I'm down for that," Ari agreed.

"Well, let me save this, and you can start working on the next track for the album," he smiled.

Half-an-hour later, as Ari was working on her lyrics for her next song, the two of them heard footsteps coming down the stairs.

"Who's that?" Ari mouthed out.

"Take a guess," Kaiden spoke aloud.

Jada reached the final step and shook her head and sucked her teeth.

"Girl, why are you always here? Don't you got a job?" Jada asked.

Ari didn't reply nor did she take her focus away from her writing.

"On a Sunday?" Kaiden asked in a calm tone.

"Why are you defending her?" Jada asked Kaiden.

Ari began to rise to her feet.

"Because you're over here tripping over absolutely nothing. You just did this shit a few weeks ago," Kaiden's aggression rose. "No, Ari, sit down. We're going to finish what we were doing."

Kaiden would never hit a woman, and Jada knew this, so she would often test his limits. She got in his face and started screaming.

"You spend more time with this bitch than you do me," she accused.

"Who's fault is that?" he asked. "I've invited you over to sit with me while I work in the studio, and I've even invited you out on numerous occasions following my studio sessions. Me and Ari, we're down here working. Trying to make some shit happen for all of us."

"Tell her ass to get a regular job," Jada shouted as she walked towards Ari. "Then, we'll be better off. I'm sure your male artists are just as solid."

In an instant, Jada grabbed the notebook that Ari was writing in and began to tear pages out of it.

"Bullshit ass lyrics," she antagonized.

Ari quickly rose to her feet and pushed Jada.

She wasn't expecting that attack from Ari; as a result, she dropped the notebook.

Kaiden got in between the two as the two ladies started to fight.

"Not here, not today," he shouted as he held them apart.

Ari stopped trying to attack Jada as Kaiden stood in between them, but Jada continued to swing at Ari.

"Sit your ass down," Kaiden grabbed Jada's shoulders and sat her down.

"Don't fucking put your hands on me," she erupted.

"Calm the fuck down," Kaiden shouted to her.

"Yo, you don't have any fucking kids, so I'm going to need for you to stop talking to me like I'm one of your children. Change that goddamn tone."

"I don't have children, but I don't need a child to know how to handle one."

Ari was silent but furious that Jada had just done what she did.

"It's cool. Let me go text one of *my* hoes then, maybe they'll appreciate a bitch." Jada pulled out her phone.

"Jada, get out," Kaiden pointed to the door. "Me and you, we're through," Kaiden spoke.

"So we're done over this bitch?" Jada asserted.

"No, we're done because you don't know how to control your fucking temper. All these insecurities and jealousy. You knew damn well who I was and what I did when we first met, so save that pity shit for someone else."

"So you're just quitting on me?" Jada softened her tone.

"No, I'm not quitting at all. *You* did this."

Jada looked around and removed Kaiden's key from her pocket. She slammed it down on the mixer.

"Alright then," Jada shook her head. "I hope you two have fun together," she spoke before moving the levels on the mixer and readjusting his settings.

"Get the fuck out," Kaiden shouted.

Jada ran up the stairs and slammed the door to Kaiden's home behind her.

Moments of complete silence passed by before he spoke again.

"I'm sorry, Ari," Kaiden apologized on Jada's behalf.

"You don't have to apologize to me. That's one reason I'm not dating anyone," she laughed. "Insecurities will drive you insane."

"Tell me something I don't know," Kaiden spoke as he readjusted the settings on the mixer.

Ari assisted him in resetting the sliders and knobs to their previous positions.

"Let's continue with what we were doing," Kaiden suggested once they finished readjusting the mixer.

Kaiden looked at his phone and was surprised to see a text from Samantha.

Samantha: Kaiden, we have to talk

Kaiden wondered what was going on with Samantha as Ari retrieved the paper from the floor and sat down. He decided to reply to her text before he put his phone in airplane mode.

Kaiden: I'll call you in a bit

She immediately replied.

Samantha: No, it has to be in person. I'm on my way to Chicago.

Kaiden was confused as to what was going on with Samantha and why she needed to come to Chicago to discuss.

The two had seen each other about two months earlier when Kaiden hosted the 'Holiday Toy Drive' for the children's store in his area.

It was a way to give back to the community; not only was he hosting the toy drive, but he gave a thousand dollars from his company to five lucky families.

Kaiden: Okay. When will you be here?
Samantha: My flight is about to take off now. Be there in about 5 hrs.
Kaiden: Okay. I'll pick you up from the airport. See you soon
Samantha: I'll call you when I land.

Kaiden put his phone in 'Do Not Disturb' mode instead of airplane mode so that if anyone needed to reach him in an emergency, he would be notified.

The fact that Samantha was on her way had him a little psyched out. He didn't know what to expect upon her arrival.

"Kai, read over this and tell me what you think," Ari spoke.

She handed him the sheet that Jada ripped out of the notebook. As Kaiden read over the lyrics, he was a little surprised.

"This isn't the Ari I know and love," he joked. "There's so much hate and animosity in these lyrics."

"You've always told me to dig deep and write what's within. Ari Love has always sung about the beauty of relationships; but never about the bad side."

"Hey, I won't knock your hustle," Kaiden chuckled. "You do you, baby girl," he continued to read the lyrics. "I just gotta hear how it sounds when you record this."

"You know I'll lay it down," she joked. "Just worry about the music to go behind these golden vocals. I'm thinking of something slow, yet a little upbeat."

"Shit, I got about 3 more hours, if you wanna try to put something down today," Kaiden spoke as he looked at the clock.

"I'm just waiting on you, Mr. Producer," Ari put her hair into a ponytail.

Kaiden put on his headphones and began to produce the beat to go with the new song Ari had in mind. Ari sat in her chair and began to mentally visualize how she wanted the song to sound.

Kaiden had a good grasp of separating his problems from his work, and this amazed Ari. She didn't expect him to continue working after what had just happened with Jada.

Kaiden had a different agenda. He channeled his anger into his work. He wasn't going to make an angry song, but instead of showing his hurt, he would just allow his work to reflect all of his emotions.

***

Kaiden's alarm on his phone went off as he felt the vibration.

"Damn, three hours have already passed?" he asked as he removed his headphones.

Ari was on the lounge chair with a pencil and the notebook in her hand. She'd fallen asleep in the middle of writing a word.

Kaiden smiled. He was glad that his studio felt like a home to his artists.

"Ari," he whispered as he tapped her.

She slowly woke up and looked at the clock.

Kaiden emitted a small chuckle.

"I gotta get going," he replied. "Let's pick this up later."

She rose from the chair and stretched.

"I can't believe it's already evening," Ari chuckled. "I guess that I won't be sleeping tonight."

"Perfect," Kaiden chuckled. "That gives you more time to work."

"Shut up," Ari laughed as she put on her coat and walked up the stairs.

Kaiden made sure he saved the track he was working on and escorted Ari up the stairs and to her vehicle.

"I'll call you later," Kaiden spoke to Ari.

Ari pulled off and Kaiden walked back towards the house.

He walked into his home and walked to his guest room. He was going to let Samantha stay at his place so that she wouldn't have to spend money on a hotel; he was certain that she wasn't coming to speak to him, just to turn back around and go home.

Once he made the room presentable and did a little tidying up around the house, he headed out of the door.

***

Kaiden arrived at the airport and began to circle the terminal.

The memories of this airport were all too familiar to him. It brought back the thoughts and memories of Christina and when he'd first picked her up. The fact that he was picking up Samantha reminded him of the situation to the fullest.

As he drove around for the fifth time, his phone rang.

"Hello?" he answered.

"I'm here, Kai," Samantha spoke.

He enjoyed hearing Samantha's voice, and after what transpired with Jada, he felt a sense of comfort in hearing her.

"I'm coming out of door 7, right by where all the buses are," Samantha finished.

"I'm coming around right now," Kaiden spoke as he approached the door.

Kaiden parked the vehicle and waited for Samantha to arrive.

Samantha walked up to the car and Kaiden put on his hazard lights.

Kaiden exited the vehicle and walked over to Samantha.

"Sammy Sam," he spoke with a chuckle as he grabbed her suitcase and put it in the trunk.

"Hey, Kai," she smiled as she kissed him on the cheek.

"What's going on with you?" he asked as they got in the car.

"Quite a bit," she spoke. "We got a lot to talk about," she replied.

"That's cool," Kaiden spoke. "Maybe you can help me with this head of mine," Kaiden spoke as he ran his hands through his mini afro. "I'm going to get a cut, but I'd like if you could shampoo and condition it for me. Lowkey, I just want you to massage my scalp."

"That could work. I didn't want to say anything, but you need something done to this mess," she laughed. "I see you're keeping this car clean."

"Hush, Child," Kaiden chuckled. "You're funny; I keep both of the cars clean," he laughed.

Kaiden decided that once he moved out and was on his own, it would be a good investment to purchase a second car. This time, he'd purchased a new Acura NSX.

"You want to get something to eat?" he asked her.

"Maybe after I get checked into my hotel."

"Nope," he immediately rebutted. "Cancel that reservation. No need for that when you can stay with me."

Samantha sighed. She knew there was no point in arguing with Kaiden over something like this.

"Okay, well if I cancel the reservation, you have to let me cook for you," Samantha negotiated.

"Damn," Kaiden replied. "Well, I'm not prepared to die, so you probably shouldn't cancel that reservation," he joked.

Samantha gave him another kiss on the cheek as he drove on the expressway.

"You got jokes, I see," she replied. "I hope you got groceries at home that I can cook with."

"Nah, I don't eat groceries," he looked at Samantha and she burst into laughter at his innuendo.

"Shut up, Kaiden," she laughed.

"Man, I love your smile," he responded.

Kaiden remembered the last time he and Samantha were together and the encounter.

"Why do we keep doing this?" he asked Samantha as she rubbed his body.

"Shhh," she spoke as she licked on his abs.

Kaiden let out a soft moan as he ran his hands through her hair.

"You know you wanted it," she spoke as she brought her face up. "Plus, you're currently single, so why not?"

Kaiden shrugged his shoulders.

"That's one thing I admire about you, Kai," Samantha added. "You're respectful. Now you know there's no way I would do anything with you, nor would you do anything with me, if you were in a relationship."

"Things are getting rocky with Jada," Kaiden answered. "She's so damn demanding and controlling. And with my line of work, I don't have time for that shit," Kaiden spoke as Samantha laid her head on his arm.

"I hope you're not just using me as a temporary pleasure," Samantha laughed. "You know I'm sensitive."

"Don't I know it? I think the neighbors know it too from the way you were yelling and screaming my name," Kaiden finished. He passionately kissed Samantha before continuing. "Plus, you know that you aren't a 'temporary pleasure' to me. It's only weird because you and Tina are best friends. Otherwise, I would have wifed you up some time ago," he laughed.

"Don't try to make me fall in love and don't you fall in love," Samantha chuckled as she rubbed his chest.

"Too late for that," he suggested.

"What do you mean?" she asked.

"Nothing," he replied.

Kaiden arrived home and opened Samantha's door. He helped her out of the car before retrieving her suitcase from the trunk.

"I'm only here for a few days," she spoke. "So I'm not going to make myself too comfortable."

"Hey, my house is your house," he said as he unlocked the door.

"So, tell me what's going on," he took her suitcase to the guest room. "Oh, and you don't have to sleep in here; just leave your stuff here," he laughed.

Samantha looked around.

"I'll tell you after dinner," she replied.

"You know I'm not a surprise fanatic," Kaiden chuckled as he stood behind Samantha and grabbed her shoulders.

Her skin was as soft as he'd remembered, if not softer. He kissed her on the neck.

"Come on," he smiled as she walked to the kitchen.

The touch of Kaiden's lips against her neck almost made her fall to the floor.

"While you're kissing me, what if your girlfriend comes in?" Samantha laughed.

"You know I don't play that," Kaiden spoke. "Jada and I broke up. She busted in during a studio session with Ari and acted out."

"Yeah, you told me you all were having trouble the last time I saw you. I didn't know you all would break up so soon."

Kaiden slightly shrugged his shoulders. "But it's all good," he kissed her neck again.

Samantha's eyes rolled to the back of her head.

"Stop," she silently moaned, although she didn't want him to. "I gotta go cook."

"Let me help you," Kaiden walked into the kitchen behind her.

***

Samantha sat in Kaiden's recliner in the upright position, as Kaiden sat between her legs.

She applied a small amount of coconut hair oil to her fingers and massaged his scalp.

"That feels extremely good," Kaiden spoke and he kept his hands on her thighs.

"I'm glad it feels good," Samantha smiled.

"I may just ask you to stay forever," he chuckled.

Samantha's heart fluttered at his comment.

"What happened with Jada? You never went into detail," Samantha spoke softly as she rubbed Kaiden's scalp.

"Let me tell you," Kaiden chuckled. "So, Ari and I were in the studio making magic, and here she comes in talking shit. Saying how I spend more time with Ari than I do her, and blah blah blah. I'm not even hurting over it," Kaiden admitted, "her recent actions have made me distance myself from her."

"Sad," Samantha spoke. "But there's no telling what her true intentions were."

"Yeah, I'm glad I got out. It's in the past now, so I'm just going to keep looking at the positives. And then she's going to try to say that I shouldn't talk to her like she's a child and that I don't have any children so I needed to change my tone," Kaiden chuckled. "I'll never hit a girl, but she was testing me."

Samantha giggled at his comment.

"You're silly. So, what did you tell her?"

"I told her like it is," Kaiden started. "I don't need a child to know how to handle one. She wants to play? Okay, then. Let's play."

Kaiden closed his eyes as Samantha massaged the oil through his hair. Her fingers felt magnificent. Samantha kissed him on the forehead.

"So, you never told me what was going on with you," Kaiden spoke with his eyes closed.

Samantha took a deep breath before speaking.

"Kaiden, I'm pregnant."

4

Kaiden immediately opened his eyes but was speechless. He couldn't believe what he just heard.

"Wait, what?" he asked.

"I'm pregnant," Samantha repeated as she smiled, yet she was nervous on the inside.

Kaiden was anxious at this news, but also excited.

"Remember the last time I was here, about two months ago?" she asked as she continued to rub his scalp.

Kaiden turned around and faced her, causing her to stop.

"Well, shortly after I returned, I started to feel sick. I thought it was the weather transitions, you know? But, when my period didn't come that week, and the sickness lasted for more than a week, I decided to take a home pregnancy test, and I went to the doctor's to confirm."

Kaiden was still stunned.

"Say something," she chuckled as emotions ran through her body.

She didn't know how Kaiden would react, to the news, and she began to accumulate a few tears.

"So… you're telling me, that you have a little one growing inside of you right now?" he asked.

Kaiden's heartbeat increased.

"You're going to be a father," Samantha spoke softly.

Kaiden was truly at a loss for words.

He rose to his feet. He didn't question whether or not Samantha had been with someone else. Even though she wasn't his girlfriend, he trusted her. If she said that she was pregnant with his child, he believed her.

A tear fell from his face as he smiled.

Without thinking, he pulled Samantha closer and passionately kissed her.

Samantha didn't fight the kiss as tears flowed down her face.

"I love you," she spoke as he retreated from the kiss.

She couldn't believe she'd just said that. Although she'd loved Kaiden, she never found an appropriate way to tell him. *Oh well.*

Kaiden looked at her sternly.

He loved Samantha as well, but he didn't know how it would look with him saying that and he'd just broken up with Jada hours earlier. On top of that, this was still Christina's best friend.

"I love you, too," he finally spoke.

He pulled Samantha in for a hug; meanwhile, a thousand questions raced through his mind.

"I suppose it's too early to know if it's a girl or a boy," he whispered.

"Much too early," she chuckled aloud.

"You know, being a father wasn't in my plans," he spoke as they retreated from the hug.

"Don't tell me you're going to back out or tell me to consider an abortion like a fuckboy," Samantha rolled her eyes.

"I didn't say that. In fact, I didn't finish my statement."
Samantha blushed.

"As I was saying, being a father wasn't in my plans, but I'm not going anywhere. I'm not going to be like my father and run out."

"I'm sorry about my outburst without letting you finish. I'm so used to guys acting a certain way. I'm not saying it's right, but I guess they've tarnished the way—"

Kaiden put his fingers over her lips.

"I'm not like these other guys. You know that, so don't go around comparing me to them."

Samantha's heartbeat continued to race. Although she'd told Kaiden the news, a feeling of anxiety still took over her body.

"Who else knows?" Kaiden asked.

"No one," she spoke. "You're the very first person I told," she admitted as she held Kaiden's hands.

"Well, we can't have you and my child living in Washington while I'm over here," Kaiden joked. "Come stay with me," Kaiden suggested.

Samantha was surprised at his suggestion but thought it could be a good idea.

"I don't know, we'll see," she spoke.

"Yeah, we got time. Wow, I just can't believe it."

"Well," she looked at her bare wrist as if a watch were there, "you got about nine months to believe it," she laughed.

"Only nine?" he whined with a chuckle as he kissed her neck.

She giggled and moaned lightly. "Only... nine," she spoke in between breaths. "Not tonight," she pleaded, "I just want to cuddle with you."

Kaiden respected Samantha's wishes and so he stopped kissing her neck.

"Only because you asked nicely," he chuckled.

The two of them retired to the bed and watched a movie before falling asleep.

***

"So it's confirmed," Kaiden spoke as he drove Samantha back to the airport. "Go on back and inform everyone, and we'll get you moved out here. If you want to come further along in the pregnancy, we can do that. But you know I'm having a charity event in a few months."

"I know. Christina and I saw it when we took Isaias to the zoo." Samantha pulled out her phone as Kaiden stopped at a red light.

"Here," she spoke. "Look at this."

Samantha loaded the video that Christina recorded of Isaias petting the lions and leaned over to Kaiden.

"Aww, look at the little guy," Kaiden declared.

Kaiden hadn't seen Isaias in person since the breakup.

"He must like the lions," Kaiden spoke as he watched the video.

"Yeah, they're his favorite," Samantha chuckled.

Kaiden looked at the way Samantha was looking at the phone.

He quickly snuck a kiss on her lips.

Samantha rolled her eyes at the peck.

"You're too much," she laughed.

"Yeah… well when you have a problem with it, you let me know," Kaiden joked.

Kaiden pulled into the airport and parked the car. He put on his hazards and helped Samantha take her suitcase over to the customer service desk. He lifted her suitcase and put it on the scale.

"Well, I guess it's time for you to go now," Kaiden smiled as he felt tears accumulate in his eyes.

"Toughen up," Samantha chuckled as she wiped his eyes. "I'll call you when I land, baby. We can go over everything."

"Okay," Kaiden spoke. "I love you."

"I love you, too," she immediately replied.

There was an awkward pause between the two. Neither of them truly wanted to say goodbye, but he knew Samantha had to return home.

Samantha started to turn around and walk towards her suitcase when Kaiden gave her hand a small jerk and turned her back around while pulling her in closer.

As soon as she was close enough, Kaiden kissed her and didn't let go.

Samantha felt all of Kaiden's emotions through the kiss he'd just given her.

Onlookers were gazing at the two with their public display of affection and a security car pulled up besides Kaidens.

"Sir, is this your vehicle?" the security officer spoke.

"Yes, it's mine," Kaiden answered, although he never took his eyes off of Samantha.

"You're going to have to move it," the officer immediately replied.

"Go on, baby," Samantha whispered. "I'll call you or text you as soon as I land."

"How are you getting home from the airport?"

"I'm going to ask Tina to pick me up and take me home. If not, I'll just take a cab."

"How is she?" Kaiden asked out of curiosity.

The security guard blew his whistle at Kaiden to get his attention.

"She's fine," Samantha hurried as she gave Kaiden another quick kiss. "I'll call you, baby. I love you."

Kaiden released her hand, although he didn't want to. "I love you, Samantha," he replied as he walked back to his car.

He watched Samantha from his driver's seat as she walked into the airport.

He drove off and soon merged onto the expressway.

He truly couldn't believe that he was about to be a father to either a future king or queen. This new information had him overwhelmed with different thoughts and emotions.

He was going to be a father.

Kaiden parked his car and walked inside of his home. He went directly to his studio and created some beats for his artists.

While his system was powering on, he pulled out his phone. He saw a text from Jada.

Jada: Kaiden...

He looked at his phone with disgust.

Kaiden: new phone, who dis?

He laughed at his text.

Jada: You got jokes. I kno u gt an iphone and all the contacts back up to the cloud
Kaiden: girl, wtf you want?
Jada: Stop acting lik dat. I was thinking of cumming over. Maybe we culd make up

Kaiden shook his head at her comment. He was done going back and forth with Jada. It appeared to a consistent battle to reveal what her intentions were. He replied in the nicest way he could.

Kaiden: Jada, I'm done going back and forth with you. It's getting annoying and childish. Me and you, we're through. There's nothing to discuss and no making up to do. I gave you everything I had, but it wasn't good enough. You didn't trust me and continued to show that to me. I've been down that road, as you know, and I'm not going back down it. Good luck to you

Jada replied almost instantly.

Jada: Wow, okay. So itz like dat? K. im not even gonna worry.

Kaiden didn't entertain her. He placed his phone face down and began to work on the instrumentals.

■■■

Samantha got off the plane and walked to the baggage claim.

She was very pleased that Kaiden didn't turn her away or run out of her life because of this.

Samantha (to Kaiden): I've landed

She returned her phone to her pocket as she waited for her flight's suitcases to move around the carousel.

When her suitcase came out, she walked outside where Christina waited for her.

Samantha took a deep breath and walked to the car. She knew she had to let Christina know that she was pregnant with Kaiden's child. It was only a matter of time before her pregnancy was obvious.

"Welcome back," Christina shouted as she let the window down.

"Good to be back," Samantha chuckled as she loaded her suitcase into the back of the car.

Samantha closed the trunk and walked around to the passenger's door.

She entered the vehicle and Christina pulled away.

"So, how was the trip?" Christina asked her. "I need details, girl."

Christina was unaware that Samantha had gone to see Kaiden; she figured she was just going on vacation to get away.

"Much needed," Samantha chuckled. "Felt good to get away for a few days. But on some real shit, I got something I have to talk to you about."

Christina wondered what it was that Samantha had to discuss with her.

"Sure, what's up?" Christina asked.

"You gotta promise to not get mad," Samantha spoke as she faced her friend.

Christina continued to drive and chuckled.

"Why would I get mad at you?" she asked.

"Because what I'm telling you, you're not going to want to hear," she shrugged her shoulders.

"Try me," Christina replied.

Samantha took a deep breath.

"I went to see Kaiden," she blurted.

Christina's smile didn't seem to fade.

"Girl, why would that make me mad?" she chuckled. "You're at liberty to do whatever you want."

"There's more," Samantha interrupted. "I visited him because…"

"Girl, save me the details," she chuckled. "I've had him, I know how good it is."

"It's not that," she told Christina. "About two months ago when I went to one of his events, some things went down. This time, I had to tell him something."

Christina's smile remained on her face.

"Christina, I'm pregnant," Samantha spoke in a soft tone.

The news shocked Christina; so much so, that she pulled the car over.

"Girl, what?!" she asked.

"Yup, I'm about 2 months pregnant."

"Congratulations, girl," Christina was excited for her friend. She pulled Samantha in for a hug. "Who's the father?"

Samantha didn't understand how Christina didn't put two and two together.

"Kaiden," Samantha spoke to her friend.

Christina's smile faded.

"*My* Kaiden?" Christina asked.

"He's not your Kaiden anymore," Samantha rebutted.

"No, I didn't mean it like that. I'm asking if we're referring to the same guy."

Samantha rolled her eyes.

"Well, I only know one Kaiden, so… yeah."

Christina faced the road once again and drove off.

"So, what are you all going to do?" she asked.

"Well, I'm thinking of moving out there to be with him."

Christina had a flashback of the conversation that she and Kaiden had.

"So, we're going to get you moved out here? Okay? I want to see you on a regular basis," Kaiden spoke to Christina.

"I don't know about that," she spoke in a low tone as she texted Jordan.

"Why you seeming so distant?" he asked.

"Nothing, Kai."

Christina (to Jordan): I love you
Jordan: love u 2
Jordan: wen u gon dump that bitch ass nigga
Christina (to Jordan): I just need time

"Something's definitely wrong," Kaiden spoke into the phone.

"It's nothing," Christina lied.

She wanted to break up with Kaiden, but couldn't figure out the nicest way to do so, although there really wasn't an easy way to break up with someone to be with someone else.

"Okay..." Kaiden started, "well do you think that's a good idea?" he asked.

"I'll have to think about it," she immediately replied. "But Kaiden, I'm going to talk to you later. Isaias is crying," she lied.

"Okay. I love you," he spoke as she hung up.

Kaiden looked at his phone and the call ended.

Christina continued to question Samantha.

"Do you think that's a good idea?"

Samantha shrugged her shoulders. "It could be. I mean, I still have quite a bit of time to think about it. He seems like he's really excited."

"I'm sure he'll make a great father," Christina added. "You sure it's his?" she joked.

"I'm not you," Samantha laughed.

"Bitch, I'm fabulous," Christina chuckled as she flipped her hair with her hand.

Christina was a little disappointed that Samantha was going to have Kaiden's child, but at the same time, she was very happy for her. She knew that Kaiden wouldn't do anything to jeopardize her friend's feelings or his child. He would do whatever it took to ensure that his child could prosper.

"Do you know if I'm having a niece or a nephew?"

"Too early to tell. I'm going for an ultrasound appointment in the next month or two and get him up here to find out the gender with me."

"That baby's gonna come out making music," Christina laughed.

"Probably will," Samantha laughed. "You know Kaiden loves his music."

"On a serious note, I don't think he'll be here for every appointment, but you know I got you."

"I'm surprised you're so cool with this," Samantha spoke.

"To be honest, I'm not," Christina confessed. "But as long as you're happy, I'm happy. Plus, there's no reason to be upset."

Samantha smiled.

"Thanks, Tina."

Samantha sat back in the chair and looked at her phone for the first time since she'd gotten in the car.

> **Kaiden: Okay, babe. Are you with Christina?**
> **Samantha: Yeah. She was here when I landed.**
> **Kaiden: Okay, call me when you get home. Tell Tina I said hello**
> **Samantha: I will.**

Samantha locked her phone and returned it to her pocket.

"Kaiden says hi," Samantha spoke to Christina.

"Tell him I said 'what's good'," Christina laughed. "You don't find it kind of weird that you're pregnant with Kaiden's child?" Christina asked.

Samantha didn't reply to the question.

Christina could tell that Samantha didn't wish to answer the question, so she didn't force the issue.

"It is, but let's drop it, okay?" Samantha finally spoke.

"Whatever you want," Christina replied. "I'm just glad that you're doing well and are keeping my niece or nephew in good shape."

"I'll do my best," Samantha spoke as she put her hands on her stomach.

Christina arrived at Samantha's house an hour later and helped her unload her suitcase from the car.

"I'm glad you told me," Christina spoke as she embraced Samantha. "I gotta get back and get Isaias from my mom."

"I love you, girl," Samantha spoke as she held her friend tightly.

"I love you, too," she replied.

Christina got in the car and drove off as Samantha closed the door.

Christina told Samantha that she had to get Isaias from her mother, but that wasn't the case. Isaias was at home with her boyfriend of two months, Trequan.

Christina drove home where she was greeted at the door by a smiling Isaias.

"Mommy, look," Isaias spoke as he pointed to his Trequan. "Trey bought me this lion!"

"Wow, I see that," Christina spoke. "Is it a grown lion or a baby lion?" she asked Isaias.

"He's a big lion," Isaias roared.

"We thought you weren't going to return," Trequan joked.

"Now, why would you think that?" Christina smiled.

"You were gone from us for way too long," Trequan spoke as he closed the door.

"I'm back now, so everything's good," Christina took off her coat and grabbed a hanger. "Plus," she continued, "I just found out some interesting news."

Christina put her coat in the closet.

"What's that?" Trequan asked.

"My best friend, Samantha, she's pregnant," Christina continued as she walked into the kitchen.

"Word?" Trequan asked. "That's what's up. She cool with the father?"

"Oh yea, really cool," she chuckled. "It's my ex."

Trequan released a hearty laugh.

"That's what yall do? Yall share men?"

Christina shook her head as she faced Trequan.

"So, I guess you're going to share me?" he joked.

"Nah," she spoke. "There will be no sharing of you," she rubbed his chest.

"Uh-huh," he chuckled. "Better not be."

5

Kaiden closed his eyes as he spoke to Samantha.

"And today, I went to the doctor for an appointment. Believe it or not, I still haven't checked the ultrasound. The doctors really want to get this ultrasound going because I'm already 16 weeks, but I want for you to be there when we hear the baby's heartbeat," Samantha spoke excitedly. "You should see my baby bump," she spoke.

"Yeah, I got a few things lined up over here," Kaiden spoke as he looked around at the papers that covered the mixer. "But you know what, I'll come back to this shit later. You and my child are more important." Kaiden spoke as he went to the airline's website.

"No, babe, it's okay. I know you have a ton of things lined up. Plus, your charity event is coming up," she remembered.

"That's a great thing," Kaiden started, "imagine me doing my thing on the stage with Ari, B-Smoove, and my newest artist, Lester the Prophet, and then debuting that I have a child on the way by this beautiful young lady. That would be a sight," Kaiden imagined. "A very beautiful sight."

"I've given some thought as to what you were saying about me moving there. Believe it or not," she spoke, "I've already packed all of my clothes and things. I just have to get everything transferred from the doctor's."

"Really?" he asked with a smile. "So now you'll be close to me."

Kaiden looked at his calendar.

"Tell you what," he started. "My charity event is coming up in about two months. How about I fly out there in the next two days, we go to the doctor for the ultrasound, get all of the paperwork, and we both drive back here and get you moved?"

If it was one thing that Kaiden was good at, it was planning things out, especially when it was crunch time.

"Oh my God, yes!" Samantha squealed.

"And that would give us enough time to get you moved in and still have time to get everything situated for the event."

"I love it," Samantha spoke.

"I'm buying my plane ticket now," Kaiden replied as he purchased a one-way ticket.

Samantha was smiling from ear to ear as she rubbed her stomach.

"I wish I could hold you right now," Kaiden spoke.

"A few days and it will be forever," Samantha answered.

"Yes, it will," Kaiden replied. "Baby, let me call you tonight. Smoove is about to come through and I have to finish getting things set."

"Okay, baby," she replied. "I love you."

"I love you, more," Kaiden answered. "Talk to you soon."

Samantha ended the call and Kaiden left the studio. He grabbed a can of iced tea from his refrigerator and sat on his porch. He felt his phone vibrate and he retrieved it from his pocket.

Christina: Hey

He was surprised to see her name appear on his phone. He hadn't heard from her in months, not even to say 'hello' or 'congratulations'.

Kaiden: Hey
Christina: What's up?
Kaiden: Nothing. What's going on with you and the little guy?
Christina: Same old, same old
Christina: Lol. I hear you're about to move my girl out there
Kaiden: It'll be best for us to be together, especially since she's pregnant with my child

His phone vibrated again to notify him of another text.

He went back to his message log and saw a text from Samantha. He opened the message and saw a picture of her holding her stomach. She captioned the picture 'we wish you were here'.

Kaiden (to Samantha): ♥♥♥ *beautiful*

Kaiden went back to his message list to open Christina's message.

Christina: Yea… I've been meaning to talk to you about that
Kaiden: if you're about to talk crazy to me, save it. My mind is made up
Christina: If you say so… Let me ask you a hypothetical question
Kaiden: Ask away
Christina: if your girlfriend told you she didn't like how you were interacting with other girls, what would you do? Would you continue to do the same thing or what?

Kaiden knew why she was asking the question. She typically only texted Kaiden when she was having trouble with her boyfriend and needed advice.

Kaiden: Well, I wouldn't. You know, my objective is to satisfy my lady. Plain and simple
Christina: I wish more guys thought like you. Lol

Kaiden looked up from his phone and saw an unidentified car drive up.

He returned his phone to his pocket but kept his eyes on the vehicle.

The door opened and a slim man approached him.

"Yo, you Kaiden?" he asked as he got closer.

Kaiden rose to his feet in case he had to defend himself.

"Who's asking?" he asked.

"I heard you been doggin' my girl," the man spoke. "You know, Jada?"

Kaiden wasn't surprised that she sent someone to his home to threaten him.

"Your girl?" Kaiden chuckled, "no disrespect, bruh, but I'm not about to get into it with you over her."

"You already in it, cuz," he replied as he pushed Kaiden.

Kaiden chuckled.

"Look, man, don't put your hands on me," Kaiden was getting mad, but didn't dare show it. "You asking about me disrespecting her, but you need to be asking what she did to deserve that shit."

"I'm not going to go to her. I'm coming to you, on some man-to-man type shit," the man stated as he inched closer to Kaiden.

"Like I said, you need to check her. Fuck this man-to-man shit you talking 'bout."

The man adjusted his sagging pants and put his forehead against Kaiden's.

"You a man, right? Not no little bitch?"

"Fuck you want, bruh?" Kaiden shouted in his face.

Kaiden was furious at this point. He no longer was concerned about being captured by a bystander who may have been recording.

"You come over to my place and try to make me cower like a little bitch over your bitch? Fuck you, nigga. I'm KG. You fuckin' with King Pin now."

'King Pin' was the name that Kaiden gave to the artists that he represented and produced. The closeness that they shared was similar to a family, and Kaiden knew that if something were to go down, they'd be the first on the scene.

The man shoved Kaiden.

"Fuck you and yo clique. This Lynch Mob, nigga," the man shouted at Kaiden.

Kaiden pushed him back with great force.

The man threw a punch at Kaiden and Kaiden ducked, but the hit still connected with his face.

Kaiden hit the man with a left jab and then a right hook before shoving him down to the ground.

Byron, Smoove's real name, saw what was occurring as he arrived and quickly exited his vehicle and ran over to Kaiden.

Adrenaline was rushing through Kaiden and he truly didn't care about much of anything at that point.

Byron ran in and grabbed Kaiden as he punched the man while he was on the ground.

As Byron held Kaiden back, the man started to get up and was about to hit Kaiden again.

Byron turned around and kicked the man as he tried to stand.

"Fuck is wrong with you?!" Byron shouted to the man. "Get the fuck out of here," he spoke as he and Kaiden walked into the home.

Byron closed the door and Kaiden took deep breaths.

"The fuck was that about?"

"Jada sent her new man over here to threaten me," Kaiden replied.

"Let me find out I'm going to have to hire professional security for you, Kai," Byron uttered as he removed his jacket.

"Fuck that nigga and let's drop this shit," Kaiden spoke. "Let's go kill some shit in the studio," Kaiden did his handshake with Byron before walking to the basement.

"You got these niggas coming for your head now. Don't make me catch a case for you. You know I'd do it."

"That's not the image we present," Kaiden answered. "You gotta represent, Smoove," Kaiden explained. "I fucked up in putting my hands on that fool."

"I'm just saying bro," he replied. "You know that me and the homies got you."

"That's love," Kaiden started, "but let's get fresh and let this aggression out over this beat," Kaiden encouraged.

Byron walked into the studio recording room and put on the headphones.

Kaiden played the beat for him and he heard the instrumental.

"Turn the bass up a little," he spoke over the mic as Kaiden slowly increased the bass.

"Oh shit!" Byron exclaimed. "Yo, I'm about to kill this shit; maybe take these niggas to church. I'm gonna spit some real shit," he spoke as he got a feel for the beat. "Kai, run this back."

"You good in there, nigga?" Kaiden chuckled over the mic.

"Yeah," Byron laughed.

Kaiden restarted the instrumental and Byron started to rap.

I've woken up, no longer sleepin
The word of my Lord is seepin in
Satan's still lurking around, just creepin
Along with his army full of rotten demons
Taking advantage of people's demons
Everything you've sown, you know you're reapin
Better repent now, or be defeated
By the deceivement of your world's leaders
Hell no, you don't have freedom
They make you believe that so you won't see them
Seek the Lord, confess your sins, give your soul
You'll start breathin
Satan knows his time is short

So he's wringing this world by the throat
And the Lord revealin to your face
But you're still choosing to ignore
How much more do you need to see?
Evil is at its highest degree
WW3 is comin, people killin for fun
The way it's happening, it feels like we all gone got a
disease."

***

"You should have never let me near that beat," Byron laughed as he and Kaiden watched the football game.

"You a whole fool, bruh," Kaiden chuckled. "How you supposed to be a damn super thug, and you're rapping about religion?"

Kaiden liked the fact that Byron had the ability to freestyle about nearly anything. Whether he rapped about smoking weed, sleeping with women, or bringing light to what was going on in the world, Byron always seemed to deliver.

"I got it like that," Byron replied with a laugh.

"Yeah, okay," Kaiden laughed.

"So, talk to me," Byron began as he took a sip of his pop. "Why was the studio closed for the past week? I drove past and saw you with a female leaving out one day."

"Shit, you want me to be honest with you?" Kaiden asked.

"Keep it 300 with me."

"That's my baby's mom. Wait," Kaiden paused, "let me correct that. That's my potential future wife. She stays over in Washington."

"Wait, you're going to be a father?" Byron asked, surprised at this information.

"Sooner than later," Kaiden spoke.

"My nigga, congratulations! You know we're throwing you a party," he chuckled.

"Nah, you don't have to do that," Kaiden chuckled. "You just worry about killing it at this charity performance in the coming months. I'm not going to be in town for about a week, so I'm going to be counting on you, Ari, and Prophet to come together and get this perfected."

"Where are you going, Mr. Fancy?" Byron playfully punched Kaiden in the arm.

"Doctor's appointment, bruh," Kaiden spoke with a smile. "You know she hasn't even gone in for an ultrasound, because she wants me to be there to hear the baby's heartbeat?"

"Don't get sentimental on me," Byron chuckled. "Nah, but I'm happy for you. She coming down here?" he asked. "Or are we all packing up and moving out there."

Kaiden laughed.

"Nah, we have too many connects out here for that. That's why I won't be in town; she's moving down here."

"All I know is that you will truly make a great father," Byron spoke.

"Thanks, man," Kaiden sipped his water.

6

Kaiden got off of the plane and retrieved his suitcase from baggage claim.

He'd informed Ari and The Prophet that he wouldn't be in town, but he wanted for them to work on their performance. But because his artist relied so heavily on using the studio, Kaiden locked the other parts of his home with the electronic keypad and gave Ari a key so that they could still use the studio.

Kaiden stepped outside and saw Samantha's SUV.

"Damn, girl, you already got a soccer mom car," Kaiden laughed as he put his suitcase in the trunk. "Out, baby," he instructed her. "You're not driving. I drive you around unless a situation comes where you have to drive me."

Samantha laughed.

"Now you know it's getting hard for me to keep getting in and out and moving around with this little one," Samantha got out of the car and walked around and kissed Kaiden.

"You're only four months," Kaiden chuckled. "Don't trip."

Kaiden embraced Samantha and took a hand and rubbed her stomach.

"I guess we should get going," Samantha whispered to him.

"Yeah, you're right," he spoke. "Get your fine ass in the car, then," he laughed as she got into the passenger side.

Kaiden closed her door and walked around to the driver's side of the car. He got inside and drove away.

"You already scheduled the appointment, baby?" he asked.

"Yep. We got one tomorrow. We don't find out the gender for another month or so, but I really want a boy," Samantha crossed her fingers.

"Really?" Kaiden asked. "I want a princess to complement my queen," he put his hand on top of hers.

Samantha rolled her eyes.

"Stop being so damn charming," she smiled.

Kaiden chuckled at Samantha's joke and continued driving until he reached her home.

Kaiden opened the trunk and retrieved his suitcase before assisting Samantha out of the car.

"Where does the time go?" Kaiden asked as he looked at his wristwatch. "It's already nighttime," he laughed as he shook his head.

"Evening," Samantha chuckled as she unlocked her door.

"Technicalities," Kaiden rebutted.

Kaiden looked around and saw numerous boxes packed around her home.

"Why is it that I didn't realize you had so much stuff?" Kaiden walked over to one of the boxes.

"You should have known. We're going to have to rent a trailer to hook onto the back of my truck for this crap," Samantha spoke as she faced the opposite direction of Kaiden.

Kaiden turned around and walked to her.

He stood behind her and took her hands in his. He put her hands on the box and kissed her neck.

Samantha had been missing Kaiden's touch, so this time, she didn't fight his efforts; she wanted him just as badly as he wanted her.

Samantha moaned and lifted her head to give him a better angle at her neck.

"Right there," she whispered as Kaiden stood closer to her.

He put his hands on her waist as he kissed her.

Kaiden didn't speak a word as he caressed her body.

Samantha was already beautiful to him and the idea of her being pregnant with his child made him crave her even more.

He lifted her arms and proceeded to take her shirt off, revealing a black bra. Samantha turned around and leaned back against the boxes.

"What are you waiting for?" she chuckled as Kaiden paused.

"Just gazing at what's mine," he smirked. "Taking my time."

Kaiden took off his shirt and continued to look at Samantha as though he was a lion and she was his prey.

As Kaiden touched Samantha, her door opened.

Christina stood in the doorway and was seemingly shocked at what she saw.

"Oooh," she teased.

Samantha and Kaiden looked at her in the doorway.

"Am I interrupting?" Christina chuckled.

Neither Samantha nor Kaiden said a word. Kaiden took a few steps back.

"Should I come back at a later time?" she asked.

"Christina, what the fuck do you want?" Samantha sternly spoke.

"I was just rolling through," Christina joked. "I didn't know Kaiden was here. If you want me to, I'll go," she spoke.

"Yes, go!" Samantha immediately replied.

"I'll let you all get back to it," she chuckled. "Don't have too much fun," Christina stared at Kaiden and eyed his body up and down.

She had memories of when they would be intimate but didn't let it control her.

Truth be told, she was still a little weirded out that her best friend was her ex's girlfriend and baby's mother.

Christina discreetly licked her lips before closing the door. Seeing Kaiden in the home almost made her go crazy.

"Any other surprises?" Kaiden joked as he backed away from Samantha.

Samantha sighed.

"I'm sorry," she spoke.

"Why are you apologizing?" Kaiden asked with a smile. "Unless you'd planned for her to waltz in like that, you don't have to apologize." He moved closer to Samantha and kissed her on the lips. "We should move this party to the bedroom anyway, especially since we have the appointment tomorrow. I'll put your bad ass to bed."

Kaiden picked Samantha up in his arms before she had a chance to reply.

She squealed a little as he led her to the bedroom.

He placed her on the bed and kissed her body again.

"I want all of you," he spoke.

Samatha was a little concerned that Kaiden wasn't a bit more spooked that Christina had just walked in on the two, but the primary thing on her mind was enjoying Kaiden for the evening.

"It's yours for the taking," Samantha whispered.

Kaiden ran his fingers down Samantha's body as she closed her eyes and bit her lip. She had a slight baby bump, which left Kaiden in awe.

He laid a gentle kiss on her stomach as his hands moved south.

Samantha gasped for air as she put her nails in Kaiden's back.

"Kai," she tried to speak.

The feeling of Kaiden's touch against her body was everything and she was thoroughly enjoying the moment.

"Baby, I need you," she spoke in a soft tone.

"Shhh," Kaiden whispered as he continued to massage her while he kissed down her body.

Samantha obeyed and closed her eyes as she whimpered.

"Why are you doing this to me?" she pouted.

"You still talking?" Kaiden whispered as he chuckled.

Kaiden continued to toy with Samantha as her body trembled. She craved his body and wanted to feel him inside of her, and the fact that he was just licking, touching, and rubbing, was driving her insane. She was getting a little furious over her sexual frustration that Kaiden wasn't satisfying.

Kaiden returned to her face as he kissed her on the lips.

"Babe," she whimpered.

Kaiden kissed her on the cheek before adjusting himself to enter her body. He moved slowly as he kissed her passionately.

"Baby, right there," she spoke in between strokes.

"You fall in love yet?" he joked.

Samantha chuckled as she playfully hit his chest.

"Shut up," she giggled. "Baby, go deeper, please," she begged.

Kaiden proceeded with deeper strokes and Samantha's moans became soft screams.

As Kaiden worked on her body, she continued to scratch his back.

"Oh shit," she spoke as she tightened her grip around him and put her nails deep into his back. She dug deeply as her legs began to shake.

"Kaiden," she silently cried.

Kaiden felt Samantha tensing up and proceeded to move his hips slower, yet he simultaneously went deeper.

He kissed Samantha passionately and continued to give her satisfaction.

***

The doctor applied the gel to Samantha's belly as he put the probe on her belly.

"You all are in here kinda late," he laughed as he moved the probe around to find the heartbeat. "Typically, I have people coming in much earlier to do their first ultrasound and you're already at 16 weeks."

"Sorry about that, Doc," Kaiden spoke. "We wanted to make sure we were together to hear the heartbeat."

"Nah, it's not an issue, as long as the baby is healthy," the doctor chuckled.

The doctor moved the probe to the left and the baby's image appeared on the screen and a heartbeat emitted from the machine.

"There's the baby," the doctor spoke.

"That's my little one?" Samantha asked as tears formed in her eyes.

"No, baby. That's *our* little one," Kaiden assured her as he gave her a quick kiss on the lips.

"I can't believe it," she stated.

"Give it about another month or two and the gender will be revealed," the doctor spoke.

Kaiden felt a few tears accumulate in his eyes and Samantha motioned for him to come closer.

Kaiden moved his face closer to her and she used the tissue in her hand to wipe his eyes. She followed it with a kiss on his cheek.

He'd never seen anything more precious. He had a few friends with children but Kaiden didn't understand the beauty of it until now.

He had a little one that was about to be born into the world and he was sky-high.

The doctor saw the excitement in the soon-to-be parents' eyes.

"Congratulations," he said. "You all seem extremely excited about this journey."

"Very," Kaiden spoke. "It's one of the most amazing moments of my life. I've never seen anything more beautiful."

They saw the baby move on the monitor.

"Baby, look," Samantha whispered.

"I know you all probably have plenty of questions," the doctor spoke as Kaiden held Samantha's hand.

"One in particular," Kaiden began. "She's moving to Chicago, Doc. In the next few days... What should be the next steps?"

"You mean to get her transferred over properly?"

"Yeah, man, and to keep her healthy and all that?"

"Well moving at this stage is fine. Looking at this ultrasound, the baby is developing well, heartbeat sounds well. The only major thing is us getting everything transferred. When were you moving?" he asked Samantha.

"Like, the end of this week," she answered.

The doctor inhaled sharply through his teeth.

"That's cutting it close," he admitted. "The quickest way would honestly be to send everything to your next doctor electronically, especially considering you're leaving at the end of this week. I take it that you all are driving, yes?" The doctor pressed a button on the machine and printed a report with sonogram images.

As the report printed, he obtained a moist towel and gently wiped Samantha's stomach with it.

"Yes, we're driving."

"Going to be a long drive," the doctor chuckled. "The lengthy drive shouldn't affect you," he spoke to Samantha. "All I recommend is that every few hours, stretch out. It'll be good for you and the baby."

The doctor finished wiping the gel from Samantha's stomach and she sat up.

"Let me finish documenting the baby's stats in my notes, so I can come back and answer any questions you may have," the doctor spoke as he removed his gloves. He washed his hands and left the room.

Kaiden pulled out his phone to check what was going on with his artists and the buzz for the charity event.

As he opened his Twitter account, he saw several mentions from various media outlets.

Curiously, he opened the attached links and watched the videos.

"Producer Kaiden Green, who will be hosting the upcoming 'Guardian Angels' charity event, was caught doing a special kind of giving earlier this week," the host spoke.

The camera went from focusing on the host to a different video.

"Green was seen on camera as he got into an altercation with this unknown male. What started out as a screaming match quickly turned violent when the man began pushing and shoving him. It appears as if the charitable producer is giving more than just time, donations, and support. He's giving out these hands to whoever may want the fade. Sound off: does this video change your perception of Kaiden Green? I'm Lexie D."

The video ended and a feeling of rage overcame Kaiden.

"What the fuck?" he spoke aloud.

"Baby, what's wrong?" Samantha asked.

Kaiden rose to his feet and paced the floor and returned his phone to his pocket.

"You remember when I told you about that nigga who came to the studio threatening me? Someone was recording the shit," he chuckled in disbelief.

"And, it made the tabloids," Samantha finished as she shook her head.

"I knew I shouldn't have put my hands on that fool," he sat on the bed beside her. He hung his head.

Samantha hated seeing Kaiden upset. She took his hand in hers and interlaced their fingers.

"Hey," she spoke after a few moments of silence.

She lifted his head.

"We're going to push through this. This is merely a phase; you're not trapped in a position that will take away everything you've worked for." Samantha kissed Kaiden on the lips.

"Besides, you still got me and this little one," she put his hand on her stomach and he felt the baby moving around."

"That's true," he smiled. "So far, nothing has been recanted from me. It's just that this video is out there and anyone can see it at any time. As soon as I felt my fist connect with him, I knew there was no turning back from that shit. But if I could," Kaiden held her hand tightly, "I would take that shit back in a heartbeat."

"I know, baby," Samantha rested her head on his shoulder.

The doctor reentered the room with a clipboard and saw the two holding hands.

"Okay, you two," he began. "All seems well with the baby. I would recommend you get your next ultrasound in the next month, month-and-a-half. You're in shape," he spoke to Samantha, "so stay healthy. Your baby will love that and post-baby, you'll be in a better position to return to how you were."

The doctor flipped the pages on his clipboard.

"Drink plenty of water, Samantha," the doctor replied. "You'll thank me later," he chuckled. "Mr. Green, what is it that you do?"

"I'm a music producer," Kaiden spoke. "You ever heard of King Pin?"

"My daughter has. She's a huge fan of Ari Love," the doctor admitted. "I'm not too big on the new age of music," he laughed.

"I produce her," Kaiden chuckled. "Don't worry, the music I put out isn't like the new age of music. If you want, I can get your daughter an autograph from Ari."

"That'd be nice," he responded. "I think my daughter is going to Chicago with some friends to see you all at the charity event. I'm not going to lie," he laughed, "she's just going to see Ari."

"That's all good," Kaiden chuckled. "I could probably introduce her to Ari; she's a really down-to-earth girl. I'm sure she wouldn't mind."

"That's a kind act," the doctor looked down and remembered the appointment. "We're getting sidetracked," he laughed.

"Back to business," Kaiden smiled as he kissed Samantha on the cheek.

"Sorry, Doc, he tends to get excited when he's talking about his work," she rolled her eyes and laughed.

Samantha genuinely loved seeing Kaiden excited. The positive energy seemed to transfer from him onto everyone else that was around.

"It's fine," the doctor spoke with a smile. "Do you all have any questions for me? I know the first child can be a scary, yet beautiful, experience."

Kaiden looked at Samantha and held her hand tightly.

"I guess the biggest question I have, is what to do to maintain a healthy pregnancy."

"Live a healthy lifestyle," the doctor chuckled. "It may sound cliché, but that's the best way to ensure a healthy pregnancy."

The doctor and Samantha continued to talk while Kaiden looked at his phone because it vibrated twice.

Christina: I'm not even going to lie to you. Seeing you and Samantha last night hurt me. And now she's having your child?
Christina: lol. This could be a disaster waiting to happen
Christina: and onece you have a child, you know there's no turning back from that shit
Christina: you can't return it oenc you feel like it
Christina: once*

Kaiden didn't feel like entertaining her foolishness. He had to admit that he did love Christina, but he wasn't going to deal with her anymore. He'd been hurt by her and really couldn't trust her.

Kaiden (to Christina): Why are you hurt? Shouldn't you be devoting your time to your man and not me?

Once he backed out of Christina's message log, another text came through.

Jada: where the fuck are you?

Kaiden surely wasn't about to reply to Jada. After she sent someone by his home, that was the end of that; the two had nothing further to discuss.

Another text came through.

Kaiden saw that Ari sent him an image.

He looked at the image and saw a broken window.

Kaiden shook his head; he knew that Jada was responsible based on the fact that she'd just texted him.

Ari: Jada

He sent Jada a text.

Kaiden (to Jada): I hope you have money for my window

Kaiden returned his phone to his pocket and focused on Samantha and the doctor.

"This is for you," he passed a folder to Samantha.

Samantha gave the folder to Kaiden and he scanned through the papers.

"It's the beginning paperwork for the transfer," the doctor announced. "The baby's information and forms are in there, and there's some paperwork in there on becoming a new parent."

"Thanks, Doc," Kaiden rose to his feet and shook the doctor's hand.

"No problem. Samantha," he spoke to her, "it was great getting to know you and I wish you the best with your pregnancy."

"Thanks, Dr. Stevens," Samantha shook hands with her doctor.

Kaiden helped her off the bed before walking to the door.

"Kai G," the doctor called out.

Kaiden chuckled before looking over his shoulder.

"I'm going to have my daughter reach out," he laughed.

"We may have a spot for her in King Pin at KG Productions," Kaiden replied as they left the office.

The two walked to the vehicle and entered.

Kaiden drove off and spoke.

"You know your friend texted me," he laughed.

"Who?" Samantha chuckled.

"Ms. Parker," Kaiden spoke.

"Tina?" she asked. "What'd she want?"

"Here," he replied as he gave Samantha his phone.

Samantha saw another text from Christina that Kaiden hadn't seen yet.

"You know she texted you again," Samantha alerted him.

"What does it say?" he asked.

"'Idk why you're acting so stupid all of a sudden, as though we never happened'," Samantha paused in reading the text; it was clear to her that Christina wasn't fully over Kaiden. "'That baby is going to cause nothing but problems and we may not ever get back together once it comes around'. What the fuck?" Samantha asked. "Is this girl really insinuating that I should get an abortion so that she could have a chance with you?" she asked Kaiden. "She's so damn phony," Samantha chuckled.

"There's more," he laughed as he merged onto the expressway. "Unlock the phone and read the thread."

Samantha entered his passcode into his phone and went to Christina's thread.

As she read the thread, she got angrier and angrier at Christina.

"I see I'm gonna have to cut her off," Samantha spoke. "She's really trying to get back with you and persuade you to convince me to have an abortion."

"I'm not going back to that life," Kaiden said. "You and my child mean the world to me, and that's really all I care about right now. If I lost all that I have, I wouldn't even mind because I have you," Kaiden assured Samantha.

"I have nothing else to say to her," Samantha shook her head. "That's supposed to be my girl but she's obviously on B.S."

"Baby, don't even let it get to you," Kaiden merged off of the expressway and turned right to get to Samantha's home.

Samantha pressed back and went to Kaiden's message log.

"Let me see what you and your other hoes talk about," she joked.

"I just sent a few pics of my Johnson and told them how I wanted to slowly stroke them," Kaiden laughed. "But feel free to look."

Samantha enjoyed how she could truly trust Kaiden and she knew that he was completely joking. Still, she was super nosy, so she tapped on the message thread with Jada.

"Well, aren't you a violent little thing," she chuckled as she read the conversation with Jada.

"What you mean?" Kaiden asked.

"You texted her about sending someone to your home and how she better not try that shit again and you hope she has the money for your fucking window," Samantha laughed. "So much aggression in you."

"I hate it when people do stuff to try to hurt me. But oh well," Kaiden spoke.

Samantha kissed him on the cheek.

"Well, I'm not like them and I won't hurt you, baby. I promise."

"Promises don't mean a thing to me. I go strictly off actions," Kaiden replied. "But I don't believe you would hurt me," Kaiden reversed into Samantha's garage.

When Kaiden put the car into park, he gave Samantha an extended passionate kiss.

"I love you," he spoke as they retreated from the kiss.

"I love you, too," she assured him.

Kaiden helped Samantha out of the vehicle and they walked into the house.

"You go have a seat and watch some TV or something," he chuckled. "I'm gonna start getting these boxes ready to go, so that tomorrow, I can load up, and the day after, we're on the road."

"You sure, baby?" Samantha asked.

"I'm positive," Kaiden answered. "Now, go sit your pretty ass down."

7

Moving day arrived and Christina, Trequan, and Isaias were at Samantha's home.

Kaiden and Trequan loaded the boxes into the trailer as Samantha and Isaias sat on the couch. Christina was in the bathroom admiring herself in the mirror.

Samantha confronted Christina about the text message the day prior, so they weren't on good terms. The only reason Christina agreed to come over was so that Isaias could see Samantha and Kaiden before they left.

"Alright, lift," Kaiden spoke as they loaded the last box into the trailer.

"Damn, girl. You gotta lotta stuff," Trequan laughed.

"Yeah, yeah," Samantha chuckled. "Yall gonna miss me?"

"Hell yeah," Trequan laughed. "Gonna miss having Tina and Isaias coming over so I can have a guys night out," he joked.

"You got jokes, huh?" Christina called from the bathroom. Trequan didn't reply.

Kaiden shook his hand to show appreciation for assisting him in loading the boxes.

"What do you say we get out of here, Sam?" Kaiden asked. "We've got a long trip ahead of us."

Samantha agreed as she spoke to Isaias.

"Aunty Sam is about to leave. I'll see you in a few months when you come to Chicago for the party, okay?"

"There's a party?" Isaias' face lit up.

"Yup. Kaiden's gonna be there, his friends, your mommy, and Trequan if he wants to come."

"Mommy, can we go to the party?" Isaias called out.

"I'll think about it, baby," Christina spoke as she emerged from the bathroom.

Samantha and Christina both looked at each other without saying a word. Samantha glanced at her as though to say, 'how dare you', with regards to her approach to Kaiden.

The glare seemed to pierce through Christina's soul, and she felt the need to say something.

"Sam, look, I was wrong," Christina admitted that she understood the error in her ways. "I'm very happy for you, truth be told, because I know who the baby's father is." She looked over to Kaiden. "He's a great man."

Christina's voice softened. "Bring it in," she motioned for Samantha to hug her.

Samantha gave her a hug and Christina continued.

"Things are going to be different around here now that you're leaving. Have a safe trip, okay?" Christina softly uttered.

"We'll do our best," Samantha assured her. "I love you," she spoke.

"I love you, too," Christina replied.

Samantha released the hug and picked up Isaias.

"See you later, Isaias," Samantha spoke.

"You're leaving now?" Isaias asked.

"Yeah, baby, I gotta go now. But I'll see you really soon, okay?"

"Okay," he replied.

Samantha put Isaias down and he walked over to Kaiden.

"Hey, little man," Kaiden squatted down.

"You have to leave, too?" Isaias asked.

"Yeah, man. I gotta get home before all the cars get on the street," Kaiden replied.

"Oh," Isaias spoke.

It was apparent to Kaiden that he was upset.

"Tell you what," Kaiden removed his chain from his neck. "You hold on to this for me. And when you come to Chicago, we'll spend the whole day together. How does that sound?" Kaiden asked.

"That sounds like fun," he spoke.

"Give me some dap for the road," Kaiden said.

He and Isaias did their special handshake as Kaiden rose to his feet.

"Well, Tina. I guess I'll be seeing you around. Remember what we spoke about," he reminded her. "I want you to give serious thought to it."

He gave Christina a quick hug and gave Trequan another handshake.

Samantha left out of the door holding only her phone and purse.

Kaiden followed Samantha. Isaias walked to the door behind them.

"Bye, Daddy." Isaias blurted as he waved to Kaiden.

***

As they entered Illinois nearly three days later, Kaiden pulled into the resting area.

He'd been driving for six hours straight while only using his music as entertainment, seeing as though Samantha was asleep and he didn't want to wake her.

Although the two spent time alternating behind the wheel, Kaiden spent significantly more time driving than Samantha, and he was fine with it.

He decided to not wake Samantha so that she could rest. He walked into the service station and ordered something from McDonald's so the two—three of them could eat.

He returned to his vehicle with the McDonald's in hand and opened the door. Samantha awoke from hearing the door open.

"Someone's awake," Kaiden chuckled as he placed the food on his seat and the drinks in the cupholder.

Samantha stretched while in the chair.

"Where are we?" she smiled.

"Just passed the state line into Illinois. We should be back in Chicago in the next few hours. I had to rest, though, and grab a bite to eat."

Kaiden unwrapped one of the sandwiches and held it to Samantha's mouth. She took a bite of the food and smiled at Kaiden.

"Make sure you eat enough for two people," he chuckled.

Samantha rolled her eyes at Kaiden.

"I'm gonna go make sure we're good under the hood," Kaiden spoke.

"Hey," she spoke to get his attention.

Kaiden looked at Samantha and she kissed him. He turned around and closed the car door before walking to the hood and raising it.

Samantha closed her eyes as Kaiden looked under the hood of the car; her life was going to be different and she recognized this. She was traveling across the country to live with Kaiden.

She had a child on the way, no employment lined up, and no idea how she would manage or get by; the only thing she was riding on at this exact moment, was Kaiden's dream and their potential future.

As he checked the oil, a police vehicle drove up behind him.

"What's going on here?" the first officer asked as he emerged from the car.

Kaiden turned around to the voice.

"Just checking my oil, Officer," Kaiden replied as he turned around and closed the hood.

"Hey, boy, don't turn away from me," the officer spoke.

"Boy?" Kaiden asked as he looked at the officer. "I don't believe my mother named me that."

"I don't give a damn what she named you," the officer replied. "For the next moments with me, I'll be referring to you as 'boy'. You got that, *boy*?" the officer was in Kaiden's face.

"Again," Kaiden didn't back down, "that's not my name and I don't appreciate your tone right now."

"Smartass, huh?" the officer chuckled. He grabbed Kaiden's arm and slammed him on the hood of the vehicle.

The impact caused Samantha to open her eyes and she saw the officer holding Kaiden.

She opened the car door.

"Get the fuck back in the car," the officer shouted to Samantha as he kept one hand on Kaiden and the other on his gun.

"Aye, man, don't talk to my girl like that," Kaiden spoke.

"I don't give a damn who she is, boy," the officer replied.

"I'm not your fuckin' boy," Kaiden shouted.

The second officer in the vehicle looked away from the laptop and saw his partner handling Kaiden and heard the way he was speaking to the two of them.

"Officer Wiley, you are out of line," he spoke as he exited the vehicle.

"Griffin, stand down," Officer Wiley spoke to his partner.

He placed handcuffs on Kaiden before proceeding.

"You got any ID on you, boy?" he asked Kaiden as he began to grab at his pockets with one hand.

Kaiden didn't reply as the anger grew inside of him.

Officer Wiley slammed Kaiden to the ground.

"What the fuck?" Kaiden shouted as he hit the concrete.

"Fuckin' nigger," Wiley spoke in disgust.

"Oh, so I'm a nigger now? It's cool," Kaiden shook his head while in handcuffs on the ground.

He tried his hardest to remain calm during the ordeal, for the safety of Samantha and his unborn child. If she weren't around, he would have fought back or resisted to some extent.

Samantha sat in the car and texted Christina.

Samantha: the cops have Kaiden in cuffs on the and he didn't even do shit

Christina looked at her phone and remembered the time they were stopped by the police.

She had a flashback of the conversation they had following the Mike Brown incident.

"If you had done what they said, you wouldn't have been in that situation," Christina spoke to Kaiden.

"What the hell you mean?" Kaiden asked her.

"I am so tired of people trying to get pity. And for what? You don't follow the law, you suffer the consequences from the police. I know a few cops that aren't bad at all. My uncle is a cop."

Kaiden chuckled at her ignorance.

"You know, because it's in your blood, your son is light-skinned. And I mean super light; some people would think he's a white baby," Kaiden laughed. "You better pray to God that your son doesn't become darker like his father. He's going to experience the same injustices that black males all over America face."

"No he won't," Christina defended, "because I'll pop him in his shit if he doesn't listen to anyone with authority. Shit, if they respect him, he better respect them."

"You're so damn ignorant," Kaiden spoke as he drove his jeep and made a left turn. "I feel bad for you. I do," he shook his head.

"Black people need to stop trying to gain pity," she spoke.

"What the fuck? You're black," Kaiden spoke. "How are you gonna say some dumb shit like that?"

Christina shouted in her phone.

"Because you're a dumbass."

Surely, that response made no sense, but she didn't care. She knew that Kaiden won that argument.

"Oh, I'm a dumbass, but you're acting like a bitter old racist white woman who was born in a black woman's body."

Christina came back to reality and replied to Samantha's text.

Christina: this shit happened when we were dating. Get out the car and ask them what's going on
Samantha: I just did a minute ago and they demanded I get back in the car.
Christina: record it on video and send it to someone in case they try to delete it. Make sure you get their name and badge numbers

Samantha recorded the interaction as her eyes filled with tears. She feared for their safety, primarily Kaiden's at that moment.

"Kaiden Green," Officer Griffin spoke as Kaiden laid on the ground.

Kaiden didn't reply.

"Music producer, songwriter, rapper. No prior arrests, very few tickets, no warrants. He's clean," Officer Griffin stated as he walked back to the police vehicle.

"Get your ass up," Officer Wiley spoke as he jerked Kaiden by the arm and stood him up.

Officer Wiley removed the handcuffs from Kaiden before continuing.

"You're one of those thug rappers, I know it."

Kaiden didn't reply to Officer Wiley's comments.

"You're lucky," he shook his head. "Take your ass on," he held out Kaiden's license.

Kaiden took his license and returned it to his pocket.

Kaiden rubbed his wrists before walking back to the vehicle.

Samantha got out of the vehicle and ran over to him. She embraced him and he accepted.

"Baby," Samantha started to cry, "let me see you," she saw the scratches on his face.

"Fuckin' pig," she shouted to Officer Wiley.

He emerged from the vehicle once he heard Samantha and walked over to her truck.

"You got something to say?" he asked her.

Kaiden stood in front of Samantha as he was face-to-face with Officer Wiley.

"What? You gonna take away our first amendment rights?" Kaiden eyed him up and down as Officer Griffin emerged from the vehicle.

Officer Wiley was silent as he sucked his teeth.

"You're a goddamn coward," Kaiden shook his head. "You're that bullied kid who became an overcompensated cop who abuses his power."

Officer Wiley didn't like the fact that Kaiden was making him seem weak but instead taking the risk of being recorded further, he only spoke.

"Pack up your shit, get in your vehicle, and get the fuck out of here. Or I will make your day 100 times worse."

"You've already done that shit," Kaiden spoke. "I guarantee if you didn't have that gun and you tried some shit, I would have whooped your ass."

"Threatening a cop," Officer Wiley spoke. "Boy, I should take your ass down right now for talking to me like that."

"Kaiden, come on," Samantha whispered to him.

"Don't back down now," Officer Wiley spoke to Samantha. "Say that shit you were saying a moment ago."

"You're a fucking pig," Kaiden immediately replied. "That's what's real. You need to reevaluate your life."

Kaiden turned around and walked Samantha to the car. He opened the passenger door and returned to the driver's side.

Officer Wiley stood there in disbelief. He couldn't say or do anything in response to what Kaiden had just said to him.

Kaiden got in the driver's seat and drove off.

Kaiden merged onto the expressway; the drive was silent. Samantha kept her hand on Kaiden's, which rested atop the gear selector.

Samantha stroked his hand with her fingers.

Kaiden knew exactly how he was going to handle the situation and he called Byron.

"What's good?" Byron answered.

"Smoove, I'm on my way back. I just got beat on by the fuckin' police."

"Don't tell me no shit like that," he replied.

"Don't even get worked up over it, but check it, I got something for the studio. I want you to arm me up once I arrive and record me."

"I got you. Let me know once you get here."

"Bet," Kaiden spoke before hanging up.

Kaiden continued the drive and Samantha kissed him on the cheek.

***

Kaiden arrived and parked in front of his home.

"We're here, babe," Kaiden gently shook Samantha to wake her up.

"Home sweet home?" she nervously chuckled.

"Don't worry," he replied with a laugh. "You'll love it." Kaiden opened his door. "Do me a favor: text Smoove, Prophet, and Ari and let them know I need their help."

Kaiden walked around to the trailer and Samantha texted the three from Kaiden's phone.

"Smoove said he'll be here in about thirty minutes," Samantha called out.

"My dog," Kaiden replied as he started to unload the boxes. "Let me open the house for you, Sam," he spoke.

Kaiden walked around to her car door and opened the door for her. He walked Samantha to the house and unlocked the door.

She couldn't believe what was happening. She was at the door of Kaiden's home; not to visit, this time around, but to live there.

"You're welcome to go wherever in the home," Kaiden stated as he opened the door. "I'm going to give you the codes to all of the rooms."

Kaiden walked her around the home; showing her the server rooms, the equipment room, and the studio.

"We got thirty minutes to freshen up, baby."

"I guess we gotta get to it, then," she chuckled. "Can't be together or else we'll go over that thirty-minute mark."

"You damn right," Kaiden laughed as he walked to the downstairs washroom and she took a shower in the upstairs washroom.

They finished getting dressed when there was a knock at the door. Kaiden and Samantha walked to the door to find Byron, Ari, and Prophet.

The three assisted Kaiden in transferring the boxes from the vehicle into the home.

As they brought in the final box, Byron broke the silence on what everyone was wondering.

"What are you gonna do about the cops doing that shit?"

Kaiden cleared his throat.

"We're gonna get in the studio. I got some heat for that ass."

"You ready now?" Byron asked.

Byron, Ari, and Prophet all couldn't help but notice the small bandage above Kaiden's eye and all of the scratches caused by the police.

Kaiden had his arms around Samantha.

"Let's do it."

The five of them walked downstairs to the studio and Samantha was in awe.

This was her first time in Kaiden's studio and she was amazed at how he'd organized everything.

Samantha sat down in one of the chairs and Kaiden walked into the recording room.

"Smoove, look in the folder and find the track named 'Untitled 3'. Arm it up and let me hear that back."

Byron loaded the track and pressed play. Kaiden heard the instrumental through his headphones.

"Shit, Kai. This beat is cold," Byron spoke. "May end up throwing Ari in there with you," he joked.

Kaiden didn't reply to his comment although he smiled.

"They show us on the TV
As killers, demons, and thugs
We idolize these niggas
And continue to show 'em love
Fuck it, I think we're stupid
You know what these niggas see?
You and me and the homies
Equal? Hah! We'll never be
Cops be harassin us
Aim it, load it
Just blastin us
Pull us over, flash us up
Then they get to askin us
Wonderin' bout shit
That don't concern 'em
Like where we from
Who we know, where we're going
And wanna know if they can come
I got niggas on all ends
They could be doctors, lawyers, or thugs
Shit, some even the police
Either way, we gets no love
We keep our heads high
Nah, nigga, don't lower
Keep my style fresh
Nigga, fuck being poor
I've been through years of that shit
Just tryna get by
Years of oppression
But still, I wonder if I,"

Kaiden continued to rap but changed his rap style.

"Can climb to the mountain tops
Hug the block

Handle the rock
While shyin away
And ducking these cops
My nigga on lock
Talkin bout choppin these rocks
It's all he got
Though they put him down a lot."
He returned to his previous flow.
"They take our crown
But we get a new set of jewels
Wrists be shining silver
Handcuffs on fools
That's what they think
That all us niggas be up to no good
Suburban boy, Kai G
But I'll still show you the hood
Break the chain, break the shackles
Shit, just let us be
Man, I'm waitin' on the day
Me and my niggas are free."

Kaiden took a breath and rotated his fingers in a circle.

Byron stopped the instrumental and Kaiden walked out of the room.

Samantha could hear the pain in Kaiden's voice during his rap, so as he walked out of the room, she gave him a long and comforting embrace.

"I want this shit pushed to radio, immediately," Kaiden spoke as he held Samantha.

"If that's the case," Prophet spoke, "let's go on and wrap this up. Let's get Smoove to throw a freestyle in there, as well as Ari. I'll get it all edited and sent out as soon as they throw their verses in."

Kaiden sat down and Samantha sat on his lap.

"Sounds good to me. How you wanna do this, Ari? Same time or separate?"

"Separately," she answered. "I think Kaiden wants to send a message with this track, and it will be more powerful if we all hit hard with individual verses."

"Whatever the case," Byron adjusted his headphones around his neck, "I'm set. Let's make some noise."

Byron walked into the studio. He connected his headphones to the jack and Prophet loaded the track to where Kaiden ended.

"Alright, Smoove, so I'm gonna queue you up, and you just give it what you got."

Byron gave a thumbs up and Prophet started the track.

As Byron rapped his freestyle, Kaiden and Samantha spoke in a whisper.

"Are you okay, baby?" she asked.

"I'm cool, Sam," Kaiden whispered. "I'll be fine. How about you?"

"I'm just worried about you. It's so much shit going on now that I feared for you when I was in Washington before I get pregnant, and I still fear for you now. Shit, if they wanted to, Wiley could bust in the house with the heavy weapons now."

"Let them try me," Kaiden spoke with a chuckle.

"I'm serious, Kai," she whispered. "These cops are out here just killing brothers, and I don't want for you to be one of them," she became teary-eyed again.

"It's not just cops. Niggas are killing niggas. Makes you wonder who 'Black Lives Matter' is really for. How can we get mad if another kills us if we're killing each other? With this track, I want to touch on all of that. My verse is about police brutality but I know Smoove is going to touch on other aspects."

Samantha kissed him on the lips and Ari lightly pushed the two of them.

"All this PDA has to go," she laughed.

"Don't be jealous, baby girl," Kaiden joked.

Ari rolled her eyes.

"Not even," she replied.

The four of them continued to listen to Byron as he finished his freestyle.

"Why niggas wanna cry
When Zimmermen kill Trayvon?
Yet, I just seen my homie
Big C murder Rayshawn."

Byron stopped rapping but the instrumental continued for another few seconds until Lester pressed stop.

Everyone knew that as soon as Byron dropped that last lyric, his freestyle was finished.

Byron walked out of the recording booth and shook hands with Kaiden.

"We about to start some shit with this track," Byron chuckled.

"Get on in there, Ari," Kaiden egged her on.

Ari walked into the studio and put on her headphones.

"So, how do yall wanna do this? Because yall know that I'm not a rapper," she giggled over the mic.

"Girl, you better rap that shit," Kaiden shouted jokingly.

Ari rolled her eyes.

"We need some soul on this track," Prophet spoke. "Just do you." He played the instrumental for her and Ari closed her eyes to feel the beat.

She started to sing with her eyes closed.
"How can we as a people make a stand
Cause when we try, they don't give a damn
Oh why?
Tell me, why?
We follow your rules and obey your laws
But you're the fishermen and cast your rods
Mmhmm
Ohhh.
Our lives already mapped out
By you, you, and you.
We can't continue to act like nothing's wrong," she ad-libbed.

Ari suddenly began to rap as her eyes became teary.
You've already got it planned
You still act like we got

A choice to make
But leave it to you, we're still hot
And no, nigga I don't mean
These records we drop
You acting like my brothers out here
Just slangin the rock
I know, this shit ain't gonna change
A got damn thing
but I hope
this song will help to bring
A notice to you
You niggas kill my brothers
You curse my friends
And raped my mother
This rap I'm throwing
I know it's not me
But I have to let you know
That this shit will never be
I got my team behind me
And they all thugs
No, they're not trigger happy
They spread love
I know you call it gangsta rap
Well, nigga, I call it music
So, this voice that my God has given me
You fuckin' right, I'mma use it."

A few tears were on Ari's face as she finished recording. She left the rest of them stunned that she'd just rapped.

Prophet finally spoke over the microphone to her.

"I think that will do it. Great work Ari," he spoke.

She opened the door and left the recording studio and Byron was the first to congratulate her.

"You just killed that shit, girl," he hugged her.

Kaiden gave Ari a hug and a kiss on the cheek.

"You dug deep with that, huh?" Kaiden asked Ari.

She smiled in reply.

"Prophet, let's get this sent off today. I want the internet to be buzzing about this track. Clean it up and release it to radio as a freestyle by King Pin."

"Tightening it up now," Prophet spoke.

Samantha hugged Ari.

"You're a singer, so when you just spit that rap," Samantha held her stomach, "my little one kicked a bit. You hit home with that."

"Thanks, Sam," she chuckled. "Wait, did you say your little one?"

Kaiden took Samantha's hand in his and they both smiled.

"Oh my God. Congratulations!" Ari squealed. "Is it a boy or a girl?"

"We don't know yet," Kaiden spoke. "Give it about another month."

Ari looked at Byron and Prophet.

"Why aren't you two more thrilled about this?" she chuckled.

"Girl, that's because we already know," Prophet laughed.

Ari was confused.

"Whaatttt?" she asked. "Why didn't I know, Mr. Green?" she chuckled.

"That's because your ass can't keep a secret," Byron sipped his coke as he fist-bumped with Kaiden.

Ari laughed.

"Yall got jokes, I see," she chuckled. "Kai, I know you're gonna do a track about it," she changed subjects. This is a beautiful thing."

"I may. Let's give it time," Kaiden responded.

Ari, Kaiden, Prophet, and Byron laughed and conversed as Samantha listened in.

"No background vocals or anything. This is a freestyle and it must come off as so," Kaiden reiterated.

"Alright, cool," Prophet spoke. "Let me get to work on this while you all take ten."

8

"Uncut Double X-L, I am your boy Cool J blasting through your speakers. Currently being heard worldwide, and I'm sitting here with the full set of 'King Pin'," the host of the show announced.

He pressed a button on the soundboard and an audience applauded.

"What's going on, everybody?" Kaiden spoke over his microphone.

"You already know who it is," Byron announced.

"It's the new kid. How's everyone doing?" Lester asked.

"And I guess I'm all alone in the group as the only girl," Ari chuckled.

"Yeah, Kai, what's up with that?" Cool J asked with a laugh. "Got Ari all alone."

"Hey, man, the doors are open. Any female rapstresses or singers out there who can truly deliver, get at your boy." Kaiden looked at Ari. "But they may end up stealing your shine, Ari. You better watch out," he joked.

"I'm not worried," she responded with her head held high.

Samantha stood in the background as she recorded them on her phone.

"Can't forget my favorite person in this world, Ms. Samantha Williams," Kaiden called her out.

Samantha shook her head.

"Let's get her mic'ed up," Cool James spoke over the microphone to his producers. "Everyone's got something to say, especially after that last track, *American Hypocrisy*," he referenced to the freestyle he just played. "You all just heard the latest from King Pin, and it's that exclusive shit."

"That's unwritten code," Kaiden spoke as he shook hands with Cool J. "I gotta get you the joints first."

"That's love," the host replied, "but we gotta discuss the shit. Yall started some noise with this. Why so political with this track?"

"Political times," Byron answered.

"Sometimes you gotta do what you gotta do," Lester shrugged his shoulders.

"Man, what inspired this track?" Cool J asked. "You got bars on here like 'break the chains, break the shackles, shit, just let us be. I'm just waiting on the day me and my niggas are free', and then you got Smoove on the track with 'why niggas wanna cry when Zimmermen kill a Trayvon, yet I just seen my homie Big C murder Rayshawn'. I peeped that you all made Zimmermen plural to throw shade at the police."

Kaiden immediately thought of his recent encounter with the police and how many times officers were in the wrong but got a slap on the wrist.

"Sandra Bland, Michael Brown, Trayvon Martin, Eric Garner, Tamir Rice, Philandro Castile, Oscar Grant; the list goes on and on," Kaiden answered.

"In that track, we get a lot of references to the police mistreating black people, yet we're doing the same shit to each other," Cool J uttered.

"That doesn't justify the stuff they do," Ari answered. "Yeah, we got our own issues and problems, but does that give them the right to kill us? Shit, may as well take us back a few hundred years."

"When you say they..." Cool J started.

"I mean the damn police," Ari adjusted her headphones.

"One time, twelve, po-pos," Byron spoke. "Whatever the hell fits," he chuckled.

"Pigs!" Kaiden added.

Everyone in the studio began to laugh.

"It makes you wonder, 'who is policing the police?'" Lester spoke.

"If a nigga like me, who has never had any run-ins with the law, can get stopped and get beaten on, you know it's a problem," Kaiden thought about when the police abused their power while he and Samantha were returning to the city.

Ari, Byron, and Lester all agreed.

"And check it," Kaiden continued, "if I die at the hands of one of these pigs, the media is going to try to find some shit to dig up on me. They gonna be like 'back in first grade, he jaywalked.' Cause they won't be able to find shit."

Cool J pressed the applause sound effect on the soundboard.

"That shit is real," he spoke to Kaiden. "But since Kai G brought it up," he announced to King Pin, "let's go around and talk about our run-ins with the cops. I'm just trying to get a better idea as to what inspired such a powerful track."

"Let me pull out the book," Byron joked and everyone laughed. "It's too many to count," he spoke. "Shit, I've never been a wild child, but since I'm a black man with dreads, I automatically get flagged as a stereotype."

"You don't even have to have dreads now," Kaiden added.

"Or be a man," Ari pitched in.

"Kai, I know you got some stories," Cool J shuffled his papers.

"I do," Kaiden answered. "I was at a gas station, right off the Iowa border, coming back from Washington."

Ari, Byron, and Lester didn't know the full story, so they listened closely.

"And I'm looking under the hood, making sure my oil and shit are good. Bro," Kaiden clapped his hands, "tell me why I get approached by this Caucasian officer."

Samantha shook her head as she hoped he didn't drop names.

"Officer Wiley," Kaiden recalled. "Asking me what's going on, and then proceeds to call me 'boy'."

Samantha held Kaiden's hand to remind him to remain calm and to just tell the story.

"This pig slams me against the car and proceeds to swing me down to the street, while he has me in cuffs. Now, it's important to note that I wasn't resisting or anything."

"Shit, Kai, you let them handle you like that," Cool J spoke.

"I couldn't risk putting Samantha in jeopardy," Kaiden replied.

"I get a feeling that's one of the main things that set this track off," he looked Kaiden in his eyes and could see the pain.

"All of it," Kaiden immediately answered.

"Ari, what about you?" Cool J asked.

"They've never laid hands on me like that," she spoke. "But the damn pigs killed my brother right in front of me," a few tears fell down her face.

"Your brother?"

"My blood brother. Wasn't doing a damn thing but doing exactly what they told him; not to mention they approached him on bullshit."

Ari had never told anyone about the police murdering her brother.

"That's why it hurt me so much to learn about what they did to Kai," she admitted. "I look up to this man. He's like a big brother to me."

"Ari, I'm right here," Kaiden released Samantha's hand and rose from the chair.

He hugged Ari.

"I'm not going anywhere," he assured her.

Lester and Byron looked on as Ari teared up.

"Ladies and gentlemen, I think this is the perfect time to hit you with this throwback NWA. We'll be right back with more from King Pin. Uncut Double X-L."

Cool J played the track and everyone removed their headphones.

Kaiden separated from Ari and she returned to her seat.

Cool J finally spoke again.

"I think we need to hear from you, Sam," Cool J suggested.

Samantha looked at Kaiden and back at Cool J.

"You must be looking for trouble," Byron laughed. "You want these cops to come for us?"

"Be like the next NWA," Lester joked.

Kaiden put his arm around Samantha and kissed her on the forehead.

"I'll do it," Samantha spoke. "We all have a story to tell, and this is one that needs to be heard."

"Although, some stories are better left untold," Cool J spoke.

"Well I'm going to tell them anyway," Samantha immediately retaliated.

"We're back in 45," the producer of the show called out.

"Let's be ready," Cool J announced as they all made sure the headphones were on and they were positioned in front of a microphone to speak.

"We're back," Cool J introduced. "Still sitting here with Kai G and King Pin, talking about what inspired the track, *American Hypocrisy*."

"I remember when Kai G and I were on our way back to the city," Samantha began, "and, just like he'd explained earlier how they put their hands on him, that shit was scary to me," she looked at Kaiden in his eyes.

Samantha inhaled before continuing.

"Being in the car, so defenseless and helpless, I really feared that something was about to happen to Kai."

"Nothing's about to happen to me," he spoke as he tightened his hold around Samantha.

"Damn, Kai G in here is just getting mad love," Cool J joked over the microphone, "but that's how you know you've made a difference in someone's life."

"That's what it's all about," Kaiden spoke. "Love is the only thing that matters in this world."

"Speaking some real shit here on Uncut Double X-L. Kai G everybody."

9

"Smoove, I'm not sure if they're ready for this," Kaiden shouted over the microphone. "We're out here live in Grant Park putting on this great show, but I don't think they're quite feeling it yet."

"How can we make this better?" Byron asked.

"Let's bless them with the sounds of the beautiful, Ari Love," Kaiden announced.

The audience applauded as Ari came onto the stage. Kaiden embraced her before exiting the stage.

Samantha took a cloth and wiped his forehead free of sweat.

"You're working up the crowd out there, huh?" she chuckled.

Kaiden looked at her baby bump and smiled.

"You already know I am, baby," he spoke.

Samantha was seven months pregnant, and by now, it was no secret. She was showing in every way possible; through the bump on her stomach to the mood swings and the lethargicness.

"How's my little girl doing in there?" Kaiden asked.

"She's doing well. I just have to find a way to stop her from moving around so much," she chuckled. "I think she's excited from your voice and the music."

"That's daddy's little girl," Kaiden kneeled down and kissed her stomach.

Kaiden heard the applause from the audience, which gave him insight that Ari was concluding her set.

"I got an idea," he spoke as he took Samantha's hand. "Come on."

Kaiden walked back to the stage steps with Samantha. He released her hand.

"Wait for my cue, baby," he told her as he gave her a quick kiss on the lips.

Samantha watched Kaiden in admiration as he walked back onto the platform.

"Alright, everybody, make some noise for Ari Love," Kaiden spoke as he stepped into the view of the audience.

The audience cheered and applauded. The cheers subsided before he continued.

"We're out here at the Guardian Angel's charity event to help them raise money to keep our youth off of the streets and to assist them in getting a good education. And if you know me, I'm all about doing the right thing, so we had to come out and show some love."

The audience cheered once again and Kaiden looked into the crowd. He saw Christina, Trequan, and Isaias in the front row.

"Make sure you head over and check out the games and all that, and if you want a shot at working with me or any of King Pin, make sure you enter for a chance towards the entrance. It costs absolutely nothing and you just have a bunch to gain from it."

The audience continued to applaud and cheer.

"Kai G, Kai G," they chanted.

"That's love, baby," Kaiden announced. "Now, before we proceed, I want to make a very special announcement."

Kaiden made eye contact with Christina for a split second. She was truly proud that he was doing what he loved to do.

"You all know that I keep my personal life very separate; although, not too long ago, a video got out involving an altercation I was involved with."

The audience chuckled.

"Don't fuck with Kai G," an audience member shouted.

"He knows what's up," Kaiden pointed in the direction of the man who shouted the comment and laughed.

The rest of the audience laughed at his comment.

"But on a serious note," Kaiden raised his voice as the volume level of the audience lowered, "I have a surprise for you all."

Samantha overheard Kaiden and knew that was her cue.

"Ladies and gentlemen, Ms. Samantha Williams."

The audience applauded and Samantha emerged from behind the curtain. They saw her baby bump and the cheering grew louder.

Samantha walked up to Kaiden and he kissed her lips.

The audience realized that Samantha wasn't a performer, but Kaiden's special lady.

"This beautiful young lady is carrying my child: my angel."

The audience cheered louder.

"Mommy, look. It's Auntie Sam," Isaias spoke excitedly.

They hadn't seen Samantha since she left, so even seeing her baby bump was a surprise. They knew she was pregnant, it was just the fact that she was so small when they'd last seen her.

"I see her, baby," Christina replied.

"She's about 7 months now, right?" Trequan asked.

"Yes," Christina answered.

She was amazed at how well Samantha looked although she was seven months pregnant.

"But, it doesn't stop there," Kaiden continued over the microphone. "I'm giving you all insight into my personal life because I love all of my fans."

The audience cheered louder as Kaiden turned to face Samantha. He got down on one knee and pulled a small box out of his pocket.

Samantha put her hands over her mouth and started to cry.

The cheers roared loudly as Kaiden got down on one knee.

"Kaiden, what are you doing?" Samantha mouthed out.

"Samantha Williams: you are the love of my life. You are currently carrying my daughter, and have shown nothing but support for me."

The audience couldn't contain themselves.

Christina was truly shocked that Kaiden had gotten down on one knee. She knew it was something he would do, but part of her was truly hurt at Kaiden proposing to another girl.

"I love you with all of my heart, and the love I have for my unborn child is phenomenal," Kaiden spoke over the microphone.

"Kaiden," Samantha whispered.

Kaiden opened the box and revealed the 5-karat diamond ring underneath.

"Will you marry me?" he asked Samantha.

Ari walked up next to Samantha with a piece of tissue and a microphone.

"*Ooooh, what you gonna do, girl?*" Ari vocalized.

Ari, Byron, and Prophet were surprised at Kaiden's proposal, but already knew to improvise.

"*He looks into your eyes*
And he sees the prize
Not only as his baby mama
But as his bride." Prophet freestyled while standing next to Kaiden.

"*He got the cars, money, fame*

But nothing is the same
When you're all up in his brain
The boy's in love
Yes, we'd stand on a limb
To see true love, transpire
Between you and him." Byron added as he stood next to Prophet.

"Yes!" Samantha managed to speak as she cried.

"*I don't think he can hear you. Say it louder,*" Ari sang.

"Yes!" Samantha spoke into the microphone. "Of course I will marry you."

The audience cheered so loud that the stage began to shake.

Kaiden put the ring on Samantha's finger and rose to his feet.

He kissed Samantha and the two slightly lost their balance because of the vibration caused by the noise.

"Ladies and gentlemen, I'm Kai G," Kaiden shouted over the microphone. He pointed to Ari as she vocalized, "my girl, Ari Love." He shook hands with Byron, "my guy B. Smoove." Kaiden made his way to center stage, "and the latest addition to King Pin, The Prophet."

The pyrotechnics shot flames into the air as Kaiden finished, "and this has been a KG Production. I'll see yall next time," he turned off his microphone and walked towards the stairs.

Samantha waved to the audience as they walked down the stairs.

"Come on," Christina spoke to Isaias and Trequan as they tried to maneuver their way towards Kaiden and Samantha.

"Kai G, Kai G, Kai G," the audience chanted as Christina inched closer to the edge of the stage.

As the three of them reached the edge of the stage, Kaiden and Samantha seemed to vanish.

"What the fuck?" Christina spoke as she looked around.

"Mommy, are me and Daddy going to hang out today like he said?" Isaias asked.

Christina didn't understand why Isaias why still calling Kaiden 'Daddy', but she felt the need to break the habit as soon as possible. But right now, she wanted to find the two.

"Maybe they went backstage," Trequan spoke. He was a little concerned that Christina was obsessed with what Kaiden was doing. The fact that she was adamant about coming to the event was a little concerning for him.

"Let's go," Christina tugged at Isaias' hand as they walked towards the rear of the stage.

"May we help you?" the security guards blocked her entrance.

Yup, he's definitely backstage, she thought.

"Kaiden Green; is he back there?" she asked.

"Is Mr. Green expecting you?"

"You guys are joking right?" Christina chuckled. "It's me, Christina Parker," she was a little shocked that the security guards didn't recognize who she was.

"Again," one of the guards reiterated, "is Mr. Green expecting you?"

Christina shook her head and called Kaiden's name.

"Kaiden!" she shouted over the guards.

Kaiden and Samantha heard her voice and stepped out of the dressing room.

"Lady," one of the guards announced. "We're going to need for you to keep your voice down."

"Ryan, Demarcus, let her in," Kaiden spoke as he held Samantha's hand.

The two security guards looked at each other and moved to the side.

Christina held Isaias' hand as they walked to the back near Kaiden.

"Congratulations, girl," Christina hugged Samantha.

"Thanks, Tina," she returned the hug.

"Auntie Sam," Isaias jumped on her.

"Woah, baby," she spoke. "Auntie Sam can't do that right now," she chuckled.

"You're gonna hurt the baby," Kaiden spoke with a chuckle.

"Daddy!" Isaias spoke excitedly as he let go of Samantha and ran over to Kaiden.

Kaiden was a little concerned at this and Christina refused to make eye contact as Isaias said it.

But Isaias was a child; Kaiden understood this, and he knew how special their bond was, so he didn't taint the image of how Isaias saw him.

"Hey, little man," he stated as he picked Isaias up. "Wow, you must be eating a lot; you weigh as much as a dinosaur," Kaiden joked.

Christina scoffed at his joke.

"My son is not big," she chuckled.

"Hello to you too, Ms. Tina."

Christina reached out to shake Kaiden's hand.

"That's all you got for me?" He asked inquisitively.

Christina was afraid to hug Kaiden because she knew her emotions weren't under control.

She hesitated but hugged Kaiden.

Trequan paid close attention to the actions and reactions of Christina as she interacted with Kaiden.

Kaiden's embrace felt warm to Christina, and it felt good to have him in her arms again, if only for this brief moment.

The two retreated from the hug.

Kaiden and Trequan shook hands before Christina spoke again.

"Damn girl, you're huge now," she squatted down in front of Samantha.

"I know," Samantha replied with a smile.

Christina touched Samantha's stomach and felt the baby moving around.

"Have you all thought of names for her?"

"Haven't given too much thought to it, yet," Kaiden spoke as he held Samantha's hand.

He could hear Ari, Prophet, and Byron finishing the performance.

"Well you got about another month before Samantha Jr. debuts into this world," she joked. "So you better act fast."

"Yeah yeah yeah," Kaiden spoke as Isaias played with Kaiden's chain.

"Kaiden," Isaias alternated, "are we still going to hang out today?"

"You know I keep my promises," Kaiden replied. "That is, if your mommy and Trequan are cool with it."

"Mommy, can we?" Isaias asked Christina.

"Yes, baby," Christina nodded her head.

"You want Aunt Sam to come too, or just us," Kaiden chuckled as he looked at Samantha.

She made a face at him and Isaias continued.

"Yes, Auntie Sam can come," he joked.

"So, we'll give mommy and Trequan some alone time," Kaiden looked at Christina. "Where are you all staying?"

"We're at Trump Towers," Christina replied enthusiastically.

"I should have known based on how much you like that fool," Kaiden replied.

Christina rolled her eyes.

Kaiden put Isaias on the ground.

"Isaias, as soon as Smoove, Ari, and Prophet come down, and we finish cleaning and closing up, we're going out. Okay?"

"Okay," he replied. "Do you want your chain back?" he showed Kaiden the chain that he was holding on to.

Kaiden had forgotten he had given it to Isaias.

"No," Kaiden squatted down and put the chain around Isaias' neck, "I just want to know why you aren't wearing it."

Kaiden rose to his feet and the five of them returned to the dressing room to await Byron, Ari, and Prophet.

10

Isaias played in the ball pit with Samantha as Kaiden looked on. He replied to a text from Christina.

Christina: I was shocked as hell when you proposed to Sam
Kaiden: why were you shocked?
Christina: idk. I just thought that would be me whose hand you were asking for
Kaiden: not this shit again smh

Kaiden didn't like to text Christina much for this reason.

Kaiden: do you not remember how we were supposed to be trying to get our relationship back on track, but you started fucking with Trequan and gave up?

Christina knew exactly what Kaiden was referring to. She remembered the phone conversation.

"You don't talk to any other girls, and I won't talk to any other guys. I want to really try to make this work," Christina spoke to Kaiden.
"You don't have to worry about me," Kaiden spoke. "Right now, I see a friendship developing, but not a relationship. But, I won't talk to anyone else to see how this goes."
"Would you tell me if there was someone that came along?" she asked.
"Yes," Kaiden replied. "I hope you would tell me if you were talking to someone as well."
Kaiden saved the track he was working on.
"I will," she spoke.

Christina shook her head at the memory.

Christina: I didn't give up. You weren't giving me the attention or anything, so I moved on.
Kaiden: exactly, so why are you still sweating me over this? You made your choice
Christina: OMG, bye.

Kaiden returned his phone to his pocket and stood up.
"Cannonball!" he shouted as he ran to the ball pit and jumped in.
Isaias laughed as Kaiden sunk into the pit and Samantha chuckled as well.
"You are so damn childish," she laughed as she pushed more of the colorful balls on top of him.
"Oh yeah?" Kaiden asked as he came to the surface. He fell backward and pulled Samantha with him.
"Oh shit," she said. Kaiden pulling her backward was unexpected.
Isaias couldn't control his laughter.

"You are so stupid," Samantha laughed as she returned to the surface with Kaiden.

"Aw, lighten up, baby girl," he kissed her on the cheek before he climbed out of the ball pit.

He helped Samantha out and lifted Isaias.

"Pizza time, guys," Kaiden stated as he walked over to the table.

The waiter brought the pizza over and they each took a slice.

"Get used to this," Kaiden chuckled. "This is how it's going to be when the little one comes," he smiled.

Samantha took a piece of sausage from her pizza and tossed it at Kaiden.

"Shh," she spoke. "You having fun, Isaias?"

"Yes," he spoke as he bit into his slice.

Kaiden couldn't help but smile as he looked at Samantha.

"What?" she asked as she smiled back.

"You are just so beautiful," Kaiden remarked.

"Are you all about to do the grown folks' thing?" Isaias asked innocently.

Kaiden and Samantha couldn't help but laugh.

"Boy, what you talking about?" Kaiden asked as his laughter subsided.

"I don't know," Isaias replied. "You all are just smiling at each other, and when Mommy and Tre do that, it means—."

"Okay, that's enough," Samantha interrupted. "Eat your pizza," she chuckled as she opened her eyes wide to Kaiden.

Isaias continued to eat his pizza and sipped his juice.

"When you're done," Kaiden spoke, "we can go win you some tickets. What kind of prize do you want?" he asked Isaias.

"The big lion," he laughed.

"Okay, well hurry up and eat so we can go play and win."

Isaias continued to eat his pizza as the two adults spoke.

"You know your girl still has it in for me," Kaiden spoke.

"Tina?" Samantha asked as she sipped her lemonade.

"Uh-huh," Kaiden replied as he lowered his tone. "Before I jumped in the ball pit, she'd texted me talking about how she was supposed to be the one who I proposed to, and woo wop da bam. Shit is getting tiring."

"Oh my God, she made her choice," Samantha whispered so that Isaias couldn't hear. "Why is she stuck on this?"

"I guess in her mind, I'm supposed to only have eyes and attention for her," Kaiden bit into his pizza. "Regardless of how she may act."

"Well, I can't fight her," Samantha chuckled as she rubbed her stomach. "Not that I would anyway; that's childish as hell."

"I know," Kaiden replied. "But you don't have anything to worry about. I only want you," he assured her.

"I know," Samantha smiled as she showed him the ring on her finger. "It just amazes me how she came all this way, allows us to bring Isaias out, and is still on bullshit."

"That's what people do," Kaiden stood up. "Let them be," he replied.

"Where are you going?" she asked.

"I got a girl waiting for me in the bathroom," he chuckled. "I'll be back in a little bit."

"Shut up," Samantha replied.

"Auntie Sam, why does Kaiden have a girl in the bathroom?" Isaias asked.

"Kaiden's just being silly," she rolled her eyes as Kaiden blew a kiss and walked away.

When he walked into the bathroom, he realized he'd left his phone on the table. If he was still dating Jada, he would have left the washroom to retrieve his phone; not because he had anything to hide, but because he knew how she was and how she tended to overreact to everything.

With Samantha, he didn't have those issues. Samantha had the passwords to all of his accounts, even the ones containing sensitive information because Kaiden trusted her. He didn't feel the need to retrieve his phone because he knew she wasn't one to overreact to just anything.

Kaiden used the washroom and washed his hands before returning to the table.

"Alright, who's ready to win that lion?" he asked.

Isaias' hand flew into the sky.

"That's one happy camper. You should take notes," Kaiden joked with Samantha.

"You are such a child," she chuckled.

"Takes one to know one," he laughed as he walked over and helped her stand.

"I'll be so glad when I drop this little one. Sometimes, I'm fine. But other times, she feels so heavy to me." Samantha spoke.

"Our angel will be here soon," Kaiden replied.

***

Kaiden looked in the backseat and saw that Isaias was asleep.

"I hope things are this precious when we have her," Samantha held his hand.

"With a mama like you and a daddy like me," he chuckled. "They will be."

Isaias held the stuffed lion tightly as he slept.

"You know that our night isn't over," Kaiden eyed Samantha.

"Isaias is in the car," she chuckled with a whisper.

"Now who's being childish," Kaiden joked. "I wasn't even referring to that. But I see where your mind is," he smirked.

Samantha kissed his cheek as he continued the drive.

He called Christina over his car's Bluetooth functionality.

"Hello?" Trequan answered her phone.

"Hey, Tre," Samantha spoke. "Where's Tina?"

"She's sleep," he sounded as if he'd just woken up.

"Yeah, well wake your asses up," Kaiden replied with a chuckle. "We're on our way with Isaias."

Trequan yawned and stretched into the phone.

"Okay, cool. About how long before you all get here?"

"About fifteen minutes. But can you all be downstairs, please?" Kaiden spoke. "You know there's nowhere to park. Plus, he's sleep."

"See you when you get here," he spoke.

Kaiden hung up the phone and turned up the radio.

"I love you," Samantha spoke as she laid her head on his shoulder.

"I love you, too," Kaiden replied.

Samantha rested on his shoulder as he continued to drive.

About an hour later, Kaiden dropped Isaias off and was arriving home.

"That was a nice proposal celebration," Kaiden chuckled as they walked into the house. "How many people can say they celebrated their proposal at Chuck E. Cheese?"

Samantha dropped her coat to the floor and chuckled.

"Not too many. But I'm sure that wasn't the celebration."

Kaiden looked at her coat on the floor before speaking.

"Girl, if you don't get that coat off the floor. You don't have no damn maid," he joked.

Samantha gave Kaiden a stern look.

"Really?" she chuckled.

Kaiden walked over to her slowly.

"You think I'm playing?" he asked her.

"Try me," she challenged.

Kaiden looked at Samantha and he loved the way she glowed.

"You look magnificent right now," he admired.

"Weren't you just talking mad shit a second ago?" she wrapped her arms around Kaiden's neck.

"Was I?" he asked. "I can't recall."

"You were," Samantha laid a kiss on his lips.

"Nah, I don't think I was," Kaiden replied.

Samantha kissed him again.

"Remember, we gotta be gentle," Samantha chuckled. "Don't wanna hurt baby Sam," she smiled.

"That's her name?" Kaiden laughed as he kept his hands around Samantha's waist.

"Yep," she chuckled.

"I don't like it," he joked. "We should name her Lil Kai. Kinda like Lil Kim, but the baby Kaiden version. She's gonna be the next female rapstress."

Samantha rolled her eyes.

"Shut up and let's do the grown folks' thing," she chuckled. Make love to me," Samantha demanded as she laid back on the bed.

"So damn bossy," he spoke and he leaned forward and kissed Samantha. "One thing's for sure: she better not be bossy like her mama," he caressed her and ran his fingers through her hair.

11

"Kai, what you think about these lyrics?" Ari asked as she handed him the notebook.

Kaiden and Ari decided to put in extra studio time to get ready for the release of her upcoming album, *Love in the Clouds*.

He read the lyrics in the notebook before speaking.

"They read well, but I don't know the flow. Give me an idea so I can know how to proceed with the music."

"I already got it," she answered. "I was playing around and actually came up with a really tight beat." She handed him a flash drive.

"Well, let me hear you. Get in the studio," he replied.

Ari anxiously entered the studio as Kaiden loaded the instrumental into the software.

"Thumbs up when you're ready," Kaiden spoke over the microphone.

Ari took a deep breath and put her thumbs up.

Kaiden started the track and Ari spoke over it.

"I dedicate this one to you Kai, your lovely fiancé, and your forthcoming daughter," Ari smiled.

Kaiden couldn't help but smile as he listened to Ari.

"Simply put, I call this one 'The Dedication'.
When I think about you coming in this world
It makes my heart sing
Just waiting on the day for you to make an appearance
I can't help but think the bells will ring
Your mama and daddy are proud of you
Before you even come."

Ari paused as she teared up and a few tears fell past her face.

She didn't give Kaiden the cue to pause the music so the instrumental continued.

"You good?" Kaiden asked over the microphone into the channel so that he wasn't recorded.

Ari didn't reply. Instead, she continued.
"I said your mama and daddy are proud, so proud
Before you're even here
I watch as their love
Conquers all the fear
All the pain in the world
You're their special girl
And it makes me wanna sing."

The dynamic in Ari's voice grew as she continued into the chorus and Kaiden's eyes widened.

"Never have I ever felt a love so strong
Stronger than superman and batman; it conquers all
I can't wait for the day that you
Are here with me
Yes, oh yes, oh yes
I've worshipped the Earth for that one chance
Now, I'm your girl and you're my man
And now that you're here, I know this is true
I love you, and I know that you love me too."

Ari stopped singing and opened her eyes as the instrumental continued to play.

Kaiden looked at her as he was at a loss for words.

"I don't even know what to say," he managed to speak.

"Say what you feel," Ari retorted as the instrumental continued.

"I feel that we got a hit with this one," he bragged as he paused the track.

Ari removed her headphones and walked out of the recording studio.

"That's all I got for now," she spoke.

"Regardless," Kaiden rose to his feet, "it's good," he embraced Ari.

"I don't want to push this until after your little one is born."

Kaiden looked at her inquisitively.

"Don't look at me like that," she said. "I have a brilliant strategy. And I'm thinking if we can get you to come in with a rap, it'd hit twenty times harder."

Kaiden gave thought to what Ari was saying.

"I'm just saying," she added. "I'm dedicating the track to you and Samantha, so it's only right that you lay down a verse.

"I got a freestyle," Kaiden thought. "Rewind that back to where you finished and arm me up."

Kaiden walked into the studio and put on the headphones.

Ari armed the microphone and played the track from where she left off.

As Kaiden listened to the instrumental, he began to rap.

I knew you were mine
The moment I saw those eyes
Shining brighter than anything
Just let me visualize
The touch of your skin, your soul, your hair
It is all so smooth
This is the last thing in the world
That I'm willing to lose

It's you and I
So baby, you need to realize
When I lift myself to you
That's when I reach the skies
Higher than the clouds
And through the atmosphere
I have no worries baby
As long as you're here
Long as you're right beside me
We can both cheer
This is our road trip
Together we'll steer
Trust me, I have no problem
Just say you need the space
I'll sit myself down
And we can slow the pace
We can do it slow, baby
Who said it's a race?
You are my medicine
Shit, you know I want a taste
When I fall asleep at night
That's when I dream of us
I combust
Not a moment in the day that I will fuss
'Cause I know I have you & until the track busts
Our train will continue; together we must
Cause, now you have my seed
A sight that makes me want to cry
We still have to name her
'I'm thinking Kailyn', let's ride."

The instrumental ended and Kaiden spoke.

"You know where I said 'we still have to name her'?" he asked over the microphone to Ari.

"Yeah," she replied.

"I'm going to get Samantha to say that, and I'm gonna put it in the track."

"That was solid, Kai," Ari spoke as he left the recording room.

"Thank you," Kaiden spoke. "Play that back for me; from the top."

Ari reset the track and played it from the beginning.

"I peeped your daughter's name at the end as well," Ari added.

"What you talking about?" Kaiden looked around as though she didn't know what she was talking about.

Ari's verse continued in the background when Kaiden heard Samantha coming down the stairs.

"Pause it, pause it," he mouthed.

Ari quickly adjusted the faders and lowered the volume so that it seemed as though the track was ending.

"What yall down here doing?" Samantha asked.

"Nothing, Mama," Kaiden replied. "Just working. What are you doing out of bed?" Kaiden asked as she walked closer to him and sat on his lap.

"You know I gotta stretch out," she chuckled. "Plus, this little girl missed her daddy," she smiled as she sat on Kaiden's lap.

"Which one? You or the baby?" he asked.

Samantha pointed to her stomach.

"She's so much more active when you're around. Especially when you're doing music."

"At least someone loves Daddy," Kaiden chuckled as he kissed her stomach.

"Both of us do," Samantha leaned in and kissed Kaiden.

"Yall are too sappy for me," Ari interjected with a laugh.

"All I know," Samantha replied, "is that you better be helping my baby make these million-dollar tracks."

Out of all of Kaiden's artists that he managed and brought around, Samantha liked Ari the most. She couldn't tell if it was the energy that Ari emitted or just another case of 'girl power', but something attracted her to Ari, spiritually.

"Me and Ari were just putting the finishing touches on her album. About 2 more tracks and we're done," Kaiden sat back in the chair as he kept his arms around Samantha's waist.

"Oh yeah?" Samantha spoke. "May I ask what it's called?"

"Call me corny," Ari spoke, "but I decided to call it *Love in the Clouds*," she chuckled.

"Ah, okay," Samantha spoke. "So you're playing with your name."

"Yep," Ari replied.

Their conversation was interrupted by a ring at the doorbell.

Kaiden couldn't use the camera because he disabled them so he could perform system updates.

"Let's go see who that could be," he spoke to Samantha and Ari.

Ari walked over and took Samantha's hand and helped her stand up.

"Another month and you'll get to meet the little one," Ari spoke.

"I've already met her," Samantha replied instantly with a smile, "but I will finally be able to hold her in my arms."

"She's almost here," Kaiden smiled as the three walked up the stairs to the door.

Kaiden looked through the peephole and saw Christina, Isaias, and Trequan.

Kaiden opened the door and they all greeted each other.

"What are you all doing over here?" Kaiden asked as he picked up Isaias.

"Well, we're gonna hop on the plane in the next few hours. Just thought we'd come by before we left." Christina replied.

She truly loved the way that Isaias clung to Kaiden as though he were his father; yet, at the same time, she hated it because she knew that they weren't together.

Isaias held on to the lion they'd previously won and still wore the chain that Kaiden had given him.

"Keep those safe for me," Kaiden chuckled.

Isaias didn't want to leave Kaiden so he hugged him tightly.

"Can't you come with us?" Isaias asked while hugging him.

"Nah, little man. Not this time," Kaiden returned the hug. "But as soon as Aunt Sam has our little one, I'm going to fly you back down. How's that?" Kaiden tried to comfort Isaias.

Christina, Trequan, Ari, and Samantha all saw the emotional moment that Kaiden and Isaias were sharing.

"I just want for you to come with us," he silently cried.

"Hey," Kaiden started, "what did I tell you?"

Isaias looked at Kaiden blankly.

"We don't cry during these moments. We smile and plan out our next trip." Kaiden tried to comfort Isaias.

Isaias used his sleeve to wipe his tears and rested his head on Kaiden's shoulder.

"Little man," Kaiden gently bounced him.

As Kaiden comforted Isaias and everyone else looked on, Jada arrived in front of Kaiden's home.

She exited the car with the same man that Kaiden had previously got into an altercation with.

"Okay, so which one of these bitches got you sprung that you had to dog me out?" Jada walked over screaming.

"Not this shit again," Kaiden whispered to himself.

The group all looked in Jada's direction as she walked over with the man. Isaias even lifted his head.

"And who's fucking child are you holding?" she screamed.

"Jada, I'd appreciate it if you'd watch your mouth and lower your tone in front of the little one."

Jada spoke louder, yet slower, to enunciate every syllable and vowel.

"I don't give a fuck," she responded. "I'm assuming that this is your son. It figures you're just another lyin' nigga."

Kaiden didn't reply to Jada.

Isaias hugged Kaiden tighter as fear filled his little body.

Kaiden held him tightly to protect him.

"Ay, dog," the man replied. "She's talking to you."

The man looked around and noticed that Byron was absent.

"Oh shit, your boy isn't here today, is he?"

"What are you talking about?" Kaiden's anger slowly returned, but he didn't want Isaias to worry, so he tried to keep it under control. "Bruh, I whooped your ass last time. All me. Smoove didn't do a damn thing but stop me from killing you."

"That's what they call it now?" the man taunted. "Put the fucking boy down and let's have a rematch."

"I'm assuming Ms. Pregnant Hoe is your bitch. I doubt you'd be fucking with your ex," Jada looked at Trequan. "Although her man is *foine*."

"The fuck?" Samantha spoke. "First off, watch who you're talking to and talking about. Secondly, I may be pregnant but I'll whoop your ass if I have to."

"Shut up, you fat hoe," Jada spoke.

"Hoe?" Samantha responded. "You got jokes, I see."

"Jada, you need to watch your mouth," Kaiden spoke as Jada walked closer to Samantha.

"Or what? You're lucky that Damian has more sense than to hit you with that fucking chipmunk on your shoulder."

"Bitch, who are you talking about?" Christina asked as she defended Isaias.

"Ah, I struck a nerve. So that's your little furball," she referenced Isaias' hair.

"Jada, you are way out of line," Kaiden replied.

Ari took Samantha's hand and led her to the house. She knew that Samantha didn't need unnecessary stress, and seeing how animated Jada was acting, she didn't even want to risk the unborn baby's life.

"Oh no," Jada pretended to whine. "Where you taking her? We were just about to have fun."

Ari didn't reply to Jada.

"Sam, I think it'd be in your best interest to not respond to Jada," Ari spoke.

"She's a grown-ass woman. Let her make her own decisions," Jada taunted.

Again, Ari ignored her.

She walked over to Kaiden and extended her hands towards Isaias. He saw her hands and looked away. He wanted to stay with Kaiden.

"Come on, little guy," Kaiden spoke. He didn't want the situation to escalate and for Isaias to get injured. "Go to Ari for me. She's gonna take you by Auntie Sam."

Reluctantly, Isaias went to Ari and Ari kissed him on the cheek.

He rested his head on her shoulder as she walked over to Sam.

"Oh shit, you put the bastard down, huh?" Damian spoke.

Without thinking, Kaiden punched Damian in the nose. Damian stumbled backward.

"I told you to watch that shit," Kaiden replied.

"You know you done fucked up, right?" he asked Kaiden as he regained his balance.

"The fuck are yall here for, bruh?" Kaiden shouted at him.

Isaias started to cry loudly. He didn't like confrontation and the fact that his mother, Trequan, and Kaiden were all involved in what seemed to be a fight, it scared him.

"This shit needs to calm down," Trequan spoke as he held Christina's arms. "What's the problem?"

"This muthafucka is on bullshit," Jada replied as she referred to Kaiden. "You lucky I haven't burned this bitch to the ground yet," she pointed to his home. "Get you and that little bastard you were holding."

"Try me, hoe," Kaiden immediately replied.

Without thinking, Christina ripped out of Trequan's grasp, grabbed Jada by the hair, and swung her to the ground. Christina got down and started punching Jada repeatedly.

"Yo!" Kaiden shouted as he walked over to try to get Christina off of Jada.

As Kaiden reached for Christina, Damian punched him in the face.

"I'm right here, bitch," he spoke.

Kaiden rubbed his lip and felt blood.

"You muthafucka," Kaiden replied as he punched Damian.

Trequan pulled Christina off of Jada but didn't have much luck controlling Jada because he had to hold Christina.

"Who's the bitch now?" Christina spat at Jada.

Ari ran over and grabbed Jada by the arms; not to fight her, but to attempt to stop the fight.

Jada didn't take kindly to Ari grabbing her, so she attempted to fight Ari.

Ari wasn't a fighter. In fact, she'd never been in a fight, aside from the small altercation she'd gotten into with Jada before, but it didn't stop her from defending herself from Jada's punches.

"Tina, calm the fuck down," Trequan demanded.

Christina stopped trying to attack Jada and Trequan released Christina's arms.

He grabbed Jada's arms as she was attacking Ari.

Kaiden and Damian were trading blows before Kaiden got in a solid uppercut.

Damian fell to the ground and held his nose. His eye was swollen and both his nose and mouth were bleeding.

Damian started to get off the ground.

"If you know what's good for you, you'd keep your ass down," Kaiden asserted.

Damian looked at Kaiden as he thought about standing. With the fire in Kaiden's eyes, he knew he should stay down because Kaiden wouldn't stop until he was unconscious or worse, dead.

Jada ripped free of Trequan's hold and walked up to Kaiden. Her eyes were red and full of tears.

She slapped him across the face.

"I loved you," Jada spoke. "Don't try to play me like I'm one of your little groupies out here."

Kaiden didn't respond. He noticed the tears in her shirt and the scratches on her face.

"D, get your ass up and let's go," Jada replied.

Damian got off the ground and brushed past Kaiden.

Jada and Damian got into the vehicle they arrived in and drove off.

The adrenaline in Kaiden died down and he started to feel pain in his face from the punches.

"Baby," Samantha spoke as she and Isaias ran over to him.

Kaiden embraced Samantha and Isaias before speaking.

"I'm sorry."

"Shhh," Samantha spoke as she wiped his cuts and bruises with a towel.

"Daddy," Isaias silently spoke.

Kaiden picked Isaias up as he cried. Isaias cried harder as he put his head on Kaiden's shoulder.

Samantha kissed Kaiden on the cheek.

Trequan held Christina as Ari stood next to Samantha.

"I'm sorry, Tina," Kaiden spoke. "I'm sure this isn't what you wanted, moments before you go to the airport."

Christina didn't reply; she fixed her hair.

"Maybe it's time that we did get out of here," Trequan suggested.

"I think it is time," Christina replied.

Christina reached for Isaias, but he didn't want to leave Kaiden.

"Isaias Malachai Parker, let's go," Christina spoke louder.

"Tina, just give us a moment," Kaiden rebutted calmly.

"Kaiden, if you got these crazy bitches running in and out of here, I don't want my son involved," Christina reached for Isaias once again but he turned his head away from her.

"Christina, chill out," Kaiden spoke. "You know me. This isn't the crowd I keep. I can't help it that she wants me back in her life after she messed up countless times." Kaiden held Isaias tighter.

Christina couldn't help but wonder if Kaiden was referring to Jada or herself. The correlation between the two situations was too real to be true. How does a guy like Kaiden get hurt in back-to-back relationships?

Christina remembered that she'd messed around with Jordan, subsequently causing her to lose Kaiden; even though he told her time and time again to let him go, she didn't listen. She'd recalled a conversation they'd had about it.

Kaiden was working retail but was on break when he decided to give Christina a call. They'd had an argument the night before and he didn't like the idea that they were upset with each other.

"Why do you act like that, Tina?" he asked her.

"Act like what? If you weren't busy entertaining these other hoes, we wouldn't have a problem."

"Now I'm entertaining hoes?" Kaiden chuckled. "You have got to chill with all that."

Christina looked at the phone at a text that had come through before continuing.

"I'm going to be honest with you. I act a certain way with you because you allow me to," she confessed.

"What do you mean I allow you to?" Kaiden asked.

"You do," she spoke. "I feel like I could do damn near anything and you'd be okay with it."

"You wanna take me up on that?" he asked her with a serious tone.

"Seriously. I could even cheat on you and I know you would take me back."

Christina came back to reality. She didn't reply to Kaiden. She'd assumed that Jada had done something similar in terms of cheating or overreacting.

Samantha held Kaiden's hand as Kaiden walked over to the porch and sat down, relocating Isaias to his lap.

"Ari, can you do me a favor?" Kaiden asked.

"Sure, Kai. What's up?" Ari walked over to him.

"Run in the bathroom and grab me a towel off out of the cabinet. Dampen it with warm water for me," Kaiden spoke.

Ari walked into the home and Samantha turned his face towards her.

She kissed his lips as Isaias rested his head on Kaiden's chest.

As the two retreated from the kiss, Samantha put her fingers in Isaias' hair.

"I guess I'm gonna have to take Smoove on that offer and invest in some security is Jada is going to be pulling stunts like this," Kaiden chuckled, although it pained him to speak too much or laugh.

Samantha chuckled. She enjoyed how Kaiden kept his spirits high, regardless of what may have transpired.

"You okay, little guy?" Kaiden asked Isaias.

Isaias didn't reply.

Christina and Trequan both looked over as Ari emerged from the home with the towel.

"Thank you, Ari," Kaiden stated as he took the towel from her.

Instead of using the towel on his face, he used the towel on Isaias' face.

"Here, look up," he told Isaias.

Isaias looked at Kaiden. Kaiden wiped Isaias' face free of the tears that had accumulated.

Christina and Trequan walked over to the four of them.

"Kai, we've got a flight to catch," Christina spoke calmly. "Come on, Isaias."

"I'll see you next time, buddy," Kaiden spoke to Isaias.

Isaias gave Kaiden a tight hug and Kaiden kissed him on the cheek.

After a prolonged hug, Kaiden spoke again.

"Come on," he whispered. "I don't want you to miss your flight."

Kaiden rose to his feet as did Isaias.

"Here, give your auntie a hug."

Isaias gave Samantha a long hug before retreating.

"I love you," she spoke.

"I love you, too," Isaias replied.

Isaias returned to Kaiden.

"I'm going to see you later, buddy," Kaiden replied. "I promise. Just keep that lion intact for me and that chain," Kaiden chuckled.

Isaias gave Kaiden another hug.

"I love you, man," Kaiden spoke.

"I love you, too," Isaias answered.

"One time for the road?" Kaiden asked.

Isaias smiled and the two did their special handshake before Isaias walked over to Christina.

"Trequan, good to see you," Kaiden spoke as the two shook hands.

"Good to see you, too, Kaiden," Trequan adjusted his fitted cap.

Samantha and Christina shared a warm embrace before Kaiden approached her.

"Tina," he started as he reached for a hug. "Let us know when you all make it."

She completed the hug.

Aside from everything that occurred between the two, Kaiden didn't allow for it to affect how he interacted with her. Regardless of her countless attempts to get with him, his heart was with Samantha and she knew as well as he did that he wouldn't do anything to jeopardize their relationship.

"I will," she spoke silently.

Christina, Isaias, and Trequan all walked back to the vehicle and climbed inside.

Trequan started the vehicle and Kaiden looked at Isaias sitting in the backseat.

Isaias slowly waved his hand as Trequan drove away.

"Goodbye, little man," Kaiden spoke in a low tone.

Samantha held Kaiden's hand as the three of them returned to the home.

12

"Welcome back to 'Uncut Double X L'. I'm your boy Cool J, please don't get me confused with LL Cool J — my name isn't James," the host chuckled.

"Plus, your head isn't nearly as shiny," Kaiden spoke over the microphone.

The two of them laughed.

"And let's not forget that I'm not swole like him."

"You right, you right," Kaiden laughed.

"As you all know by now, I'm sitting here with rapper slash producer, Kai G."

"What's going on, everybody?" Kaiden spoke.

"Now, Kai G, you have to tell me. What is going on with you man?" Cool J referred to the fight Kaiden had gotten into with Damian.

"I'm just handling business," Kaiden spoke as he shrugged his shoulders.

"That's not what I saw. KG got them hands," Cool J laughed.

"I'm gonna put it like this," Kaiden spoke. "You mess with my business, family, or friends, you're asking for what's coming to you."

"I'm assuming ol' boy learned his lesson. What you think?"

"I don't think much of it. I got more important things to dedicate my energy to."

"Give us some examples, man," Cool J spoke.

"Well, you know we just had this charity event. My girl Ari did her thing. I gotta show mad love to my boy Smoove and the newest member of King Pin, The Prophet."

"Let's talk about that. Who is this cat? We met him when you all were here last time, but I want to know about him from your perspective."

"The Prophet is a young guy out of DC. You know?" Kaiden adjusted his headphones. "After the show we did out there, young dude met me backstage like 'oh man, I'm a huge fan of yours. Let me hit you with something'."

"Sounds like a Kai G moment," Cool J chuckled.

Kaiden laughed.

"Yeah, sometimes, you gotta give someone a shot. Bruh, someone gave you a start, so we gotta reciprocate the love."

"True, true. But give me some more info on this cat."

"Yeah, man. So, I hear the young nigga rap and I knew he had talent and potential. So I gave him my email and he sent me a demo. And I let him know straight up; if he was willing to work hard, I'd fly him out to Chicago and we could do his music."

"Yo, that's what's up," Cool J replied.

"So he was out here for about a month or so, and he knew that he wanted to continue to work with me, so he moved out here and he's making a name with King Pin."

"Yall heard it here," Cool J announced over the microphone. "Kai G is making some noise over here. Making dreams happen and shit."

"We got to. No one else is going to help us," Kaiden remembered his incidents with the police, the rejections he'd gotten from opportunities, the countless times he was told 'no'; he knew the importance of giving someone a fair chance.

"Kai G, yall," Cool J spoke as he played a sound effect. "What we're gonna do is hit you all with *American Hypocrisy* and then we're gonna come back and discuss more about his life and what's to come. You're listening to Uncut Double X L."

Cool J played the song and disarmed the microphones.

Kaiden pulled out his phone and saw a text from Samantha.

Almost three months passed since Christina returned to Washington with Trequan and Isaias.

Samantha: Kaiden...
Kaiden: Hey, my love. What's going on?

He placed his phone face down on the table and continued to speak to Cool J.

"So Kai, you gotta give me a little information. What is this I'm hearing about you being engaged?" he asked.

"You didn't know?" Kaiden chuckled. "I'm a one-woman man."

"So you're not the old Kaiden I used to know," Cool J laughed.

"Nah, I've always been a one-woman man. Just because I used to flirt around doesn't mean shit," Kaiden chuckled.

Cool J shrugged his shoulders and saw the flash on Kaiden's phone illuminate.

Kaiden looked at his phone and read the text from Samantha.

Samantha: I'm having contractions.
Samantha: Ari is driving me to the hospital

"Is that the lucky lady?" he asked.

Kaiden smiled.

"Yeah. This is my fiancé. I'm going to have to get ready to head out and get to the hospital," he finished and texted Samantha back.

Kaiden: I'm on my way

"The hospital?" Cool J asked. "Everything cool?"

"She's having contractions. My little one may be on her way."

"Well, the track is ending," Cool J put on his headphones. "We're gonna get you out of here."

Kaiden put on his headphones.

"We're back," Cool J announced. "Still chopping it up with Kai G, but we're about to let my mans get out of here. He's got some things going on."

"I appreciate you for having me. It's nothing but love whenever I'm up here," Kaiden replied.

"No doubt, Boss. Real quick, let me ask what's next for Kai G?"

"Shit, man," Kaiden started, "Well, for Kai G, you're most likely going to see more of a personal side with music, production, and the shows I put on. I try to keep my rap life relevant to my personal life. That's why I'm relevant: I keep it real."

"Okay, okay. So tell the people really quickly: what else is going on?" Cool J asked.

Kaiden laughed.

"Well, it's already been showcased, but Kai G is about to be a father. A married father."

"Oh shit! Kai G's about to be a daddy? A boy or a girl?"

"A girl," Kaiden replied. "Daddy's little girl."

"Kai G, ladies and gentlemen," Cool J spoke. "Mad love to you for coming through, Kai."

"Thanks for having me on, bro," Kaiden adjusted his hat and put his phone in his pocket.

"We'll be right back after these next few tracks," Cool J spoke before airing the next song.

"Before I get out of here," Kaiden spoke as he pulled a flash drive from his pocket, "here's a track for you. All I ask is that you don't air it until I shoot you a text." Kaiden spoke.

"You got my word," Cool J responded as he and Kaiden shook hands. "Go on and get to your lady."

Kaiden grabbed his coat and ran out of the studio to his car.

When he got to his vehicle, he called Samantha's phone, but to no avail. He called Ari's phone and she answered on the first ring.

"Yea, what's up Kai?" she asked.

"Ari, where are you all?"

"We just got to the hospital. They're taking Samantha in the room now. Room 406. I'm going back there with her."

"Okay, cool. I'm on my way now. I'll be there in about 15 minutes."

Kaiden hung up the phone and accelerated.

He was about to be a father and couldn't believe it. His thoughts were racing with all the possibilities and how his life was about to change.

Kaiden couldn't help but smile as he drove to the hospital.

He parked in the parking lot and ran into the hospital. He grabbed a badge from the front desk and continued to the elevator.

He took the elevator to the fourth floor and ran to the room.

"Baby," he shouted as he walked into the room.

"I'm sorry, sir, but you have to put these on," the nurse handed him some scrubs.

"What's this for?" Kaiden asked.

"She's being admitted. She's going to be induced."

Kaiden's heart fluttered as he quickly put on the scrubs.

Samantha was sleeping in the bed as Ari sat on the window sill.

"Hey Ari," Kaiden whispered as he approached her.

Ari looked up from her phone and embraced Kaiden.

"She just fell asleep," Ari spoke. "They say she's going to have the baby any day now, so they're keeping her here."

Kaiden was a little shaky. He was so excited that he couldn't contain himself.

He walked over to Samantha and kissed her on the forehead. He then kissed her stomach and felt his daughter kick.

It felt surreal to Kaiden; this moment was happening.

"I know you're going to make a great father, Kai," Ari responded.

"I hope so," he replied as he took hold of Samantha's hand.

"Is there anything you need for me to do?" Ari asked as she picked up her coat.

"You've been more than helpful, Ari," Kaiden spoke. "You all can go to the studio though and tune into 'Uncut Double X L'. I'm going to have them debut the new track one she's born."

"Oh shit, okay," Ari spoke excitedly.

She couldn't wait to hear the finalized track, but she was even more excited for Kaiden to debut his little one to the world.

"I'll text you in a bit," Kaiden spoke as he helped her finish putting on her coat.

"Call Smoove and Prophet for me. I have a low battery."

"I got you," Kaiden replied as she exited the room. He called behind her. "Hurry up and charge your phone," he laughed as he reentered the room and closed the door.

***

Kaiden sat in his scrubs as he waited in the hospital room with Samantha. Monitors were connected to her and the rhythmic beeping continued as she smiled at Kaiden.

"Look at you," Kaiden spoke as he recorded Samantha on his iPhone.

"What?" she chuckled.

"Little Kailyn is on the way," Kaiden teased. "What's going on everybody? This is your boy Kai G coming to you live from the hospital room."

Kaiden wasn't live to an audience, but he decided to record the video for memories.

"I got my beautiful bride-to-be right here. Say 'hey', baby," Kaiden put the camera on Samantha.

"No," she quickly covered her face with a pillow.

Kaiden laughed.

"She's a little shy," he walked closer to her and moved the pillow with his free hand but continued to hold his phone high enough to record. "But she's still my baby," he smothered her cheek in kisses.

"Kaiden, stop," Samantha chuckled.

"Come on," he spoke as he looked at her dreamily.

Samantha looked back at Kaiden and they kissed each other on the lips.

"I love you," he spoke.

"I love you," she assured him.

Kaiden quickly adjusted his focus back to the camera.

"She'll be here soon, guys! I may record her birth."

"Uh-uh," Samantha spoke. "You better not."

"Why not, baby? They've already seen our sex tape," Kaiden laughed.

Samantha threw her pillow at him and he ducked and laughed.

"I'll talk to yall later," Kaiden stopped the recording.

"You are too much," Samantha giggled.

"Too much, but I'm just enough for you." Kaiden moved his chair closer to her.

"That's right," Samantha smiled.

She put one of Kaiden's hands on her stomach.

"Kailyn," Samantha spoke in a sing-song voice. "You shall be here soon, and we'll finally be able to hold you in our arms."

The baby began to move around as if to say that she wanted out.

The time was now 11:58 pm and Kaiden was exhausted. Samantha had many small contractions, but nothing continuously.

"I think we should try to get a little rest, baby," Kaiden suggested. "She'll come soon enough."

"I think you're right," they exchanged a quick kiss.

Kaiden held her hand as he slept in the chair and Samantha closed her eyes.

Roughly two hours later, Kaiden was awoken by Samantha's scream.

Samantha squeezed Kaiden's hand tightly as her contractions started.

"Baby," Kaiden jumped up to his feet. "Breathe."

Three nurses rushed into the room once they heard her scream.

"What's wrong?" the lead nurse washed her hands and approached Samantha. "Is the little one ready to enter the world?" she lifted Samantha's gown.

Samantha winced with pain as she breathed through her nose and mouth.

"Baby, you're doing so well," Kaiden tried to comfort her.

"Patient's water broke. Contractions are about 15 seconds apart. This baby's coming," the lead nurse announced.

"Holy shit," Kaiden whispered with excitement.

This was it.

"Okay, Samantha, honey, we need for you to give us a few good pushes," the nurse spoke.

Samantha's gown was lifted to her knees.

Kaiden said a small prayer, loud enough so that Samantha could hear.

Samantha pushed for the nurse.

Kaiden put a towel directly underneath Samantha's hair onto her forehead.

The nurse saw part of the baby's hair exit Samantha.

"Baby is starting to crown," she announced to the other nurses.

One was typing notes into the computer as the other stood at the lead nurse's side.

"Keep that pan right there," the lead nurse spoke.

Samantha pushed again as she screamed in pain.

"Give me something for this pain, shit," Samantha exclaimed.

"Baby, shh," Kaiden whispered as he kissed her forehead. "Squeeze my hand harder. Insult me if you need to."

"You did this to me," Samantha cried.

Kaiden adjusted her hair out of her face as she pushed.

"Okay, Sam, don't push right now," the nurse spoke as she maneuvered the baby's head out.

Once she had the head out, she informed Samantha to push again.

"Give me three good pushes Sam, and we should be done."

"Come on, baby," Kaiden spoke.

Samantha gave three extended pushes and her screaming subsided.

Instead of hearing Samantha's screams, the cries of the baby filled the room.

"It's a girl," the lead nurse announced. "3:15 AM, August 16th,2017."

The nurses all applauded and congratulated Kaiden and Samantha.

"Let me cut the cord," Kaiden spoke after he kissed Samantha's forehead.

He released Samantha's hand and took the sterile scissors.

"Cut it right here," she instructed Kaiden.

He snipped the baby's umbilical cord.

"Let's get her cleaned up so the parents can officially hold their baby girl."

The lead nurse walked the baby over to the sink and washed her body.

The baby continued to cry as the nurse put a diaper on her and wrapped her in a blanket. She handed her over to Kaiden.

She was so tiny. Kaiden had never seen anything so small and precious.

A tear fell from his eye as he walked over to Samantha with her.

"Do you all have a name for her yet?" the nurse using the computer asked.

"Kailyn," Samantha spoke as Kaiden sat down with the baby.

Kaiden didn't want to let go. His daughter hadn't been in the world for longer than five minutes, but he was amazed. He was a father and it was the best feeling that he'd ever experienced.

Samantha didn't interrupt Kaiden's moment. She could tell he was in love all over again.

"Kailyn Harmony Green," Samantha spoke with a smile.

The nurse typed the baby's stats into the computer.

"Kailyn," Kaiden whispered.

Kailyn looked around.

"Baby, look at all this hair," Kaiden chuckled to Samantha; his voice was cracking. "You are the reason for my fight, Kailyn," he spoke to the newborn.

Kaiden knew Samantha had to be as excited as he was so he passed Kailyn to her.

"Hey there, Kailyn," Samantha spoke.

The nurses cleaned up the things around the room and prepared Kailyn's bed.

"You recognize me?" Samantha asked.

Kailyn made a small noise.

"I guess that's a yes," Samantha shed a tear.

Kaiden couldn't take his eyes off of Samantha or his newborn child, but he managed to pull out his phone.

He sent Cool J a text.

Kaiden: she's here

He knew that Cool J wasn't on the air, but that was authorization to air the track.

Kaiden opened his camera and started to record.

"Yall gotta excuse me; I'm a little emotional," Kaiden chuckled as he saw how red his eyes were. "Little Kailyn is here."

Kaiden adjusted the camera to capture Samantha and Kailyn.

"Mommy, how are you feeling?" Kaiden asked Samantha.

"Beautiful," Samantha asked.

"And how about you, Ms. Kailyn?" Kaiden asked.

Kailyn closed her eyes, but to Kaiden, it looked like she rolled them as to say, 'get away from me'.

He laughed.

"She's already got her mama's attitude," he adjusted so that he could kiss Samantha. "Thank you."

"For what?" Samantha asked as she cradled Kailyn.

"For everything you've given me thus far. Your undeniable support, love, your hand in engagement, and now my beautiful daughter," Kaiden shed a tear.

The camera continued to record.

"Don't get soft on me, Kaiden," Samantha joked as she kissed his forehead.

"This is such a beautiful sight to me," Kaiden spoke to the camera. "Ladies and gentlemen, meet 'The Greens', and I'm not talking about food," he chuckled.

The nurses applauded as they finished cleaning.

"And let's not forget to acknowledge the most talented nurses in the world," Kaiden flipped the camera to show the nurses.

Each of them waved and said hello to the camera.

Kaiden rotated the camera back around as the nurses chatted amongst each other.

"So, a lot of people want to know what's next for me. "Daddy duties," Kaiden chuckled. "I'm gonna keep making music though; I have to make a life for my family."

Kaiden kissed Kailyn on the forehead as she closed her eyes.

"Let's let her sleep," Samantha whispered.

"I'll talk to you guys later," Kaiden spoke as he ended the recording.

He put his phone on the table.

"Let me put her in her bed," Kaiden whispered.

He gently picked up the newborn and walked her over to her bed.

Kaiden gave her another kiss before laying her down.

"The most precious thing in the world," Kaiden spoke.

"And she's all ours," Samantha chuckled as Kaiden sat beside her. "I can already tell she's going to be a spoiled daddy's girl."

"Like you?" Kaiden looked at Samantha seductively.

"We are in a hospital and I just gave birth," Samantha whispered and giggled.

"See, you nasty," Kaiden chuckled. "I wasn't even talking about that," he kissed her.

Samantha knew that this was the life that she wanted. She couldn't picture anyone being a better father and husband than Kaiden. He put her on a pedestal and treasured her; he kept her protected and she loved that about him.

Kaiden lied down on the bed next to her and held her hands.

The two shared a quick kiss before turning off the lights and going to sleep.

Kaiden awoke hours later to a crying Kailyn.

Kaiden wanted Samantha to get as much rest as she could, but he knew that if Samantha heard Kailyn, she would try to tend to her.

Kaiden rose from the chair and grabbed a bottle of formula.

He walked over to Kailyn and gently picked her up.

"Shhh," he tried to hush her as he gave her the bottle.

Kailyn sucked on the nipple of the bottle and Samantha turned over.

"We gotta let Mommy get some sleep," Kaiden whispered. "She's had a long day."

Kailyn closed her eyes as she drank the formula.

Kaiden walked around the room holding her as he silently rapped to her.

"I hold you now and now I can see
You're the only thing keeping my sanity

Since before I knew you were the one to me
To be the one I always knew you could be
To be what my father wished he was to me
I say a prayer, and baby I got you
To look over, protect, and guide
While keeping you away from these guys," Kaiden chuckled at his freestyle.

"Yeah, baby girl, I'm going to keep you protected," he kissed her before sitting down while holding her.

Kaiden placed Kailyn in his shirt as though it were a pouch.

She finished the formula and Kaiden returned the bottle to the table.

Kaiden gently patted her back until she released a burp.

"Ooh," Kaiden teased, "you're a nasty little girl," he joked.

He rapped under his breath so that Kailyn could feel his vocal vibrations, in hopes that it would help put her to sleep.

He quickly realized that their breathing and heartbeat synchronized, and soon they were both asleep.

Samantha awoke the next morning and saw Kaiden and Kailyn both asleep on the chair next to her.

The opportunity was too precious for her to pass up. She took a picture of the two and sent it to Christina.

Samantha: she's here

Samantha turned on the television and decided to watch the news and let the two sleep.

"And, it may be months later," the reporter spoke, *"but the numbers are finally in. You all may remember the charity event that producer Kai G and his members put on."*

The news clip displayed the four members on stage performing.

"There was a total of 25,413 audience members in attendance that day, and they were in for a special surprise from the host."

The news showed footage of Kaiden bringing Samantha onstage and proposing to her.

Samantha smiled as she was able to see the moment from a third-person point of view.

"Kai G brought out his pregnant girlfriend, Samantha Williams. Our sources say she was about seven months pregnant at this time, so we should be expecting a little one from Kai G any day now."

Kaiden slowly started to wake up and saw Samantha watching television.

"Good morning, baby," Kaiden spoke.

"You all look so precious," Samantha teased. "You're going to have her so spoiled though," Samantha chuckled.

"This is Daddy's little angel," Kaiden smiled as he gently stroked her back. "She got hungry last night so I fed her; I didn't want for her to wake you up."

"So considerate," Samantha spoke. "Let me see my baby."

Kaiden removed Kailyn from the top of his shirt and she woke up.

She began crying as Kaiden moved her.

"Come on," Kaiden spoke. "Mommy wants to see you, don't be like that."

Samantha laughed a little as Kaiden handed her the baby.

Kaiden's phone vibrated twice and he pulled it from the table.

He saw that Cool J replied.

Cool J: cool. I'm going to air it today during my show; around 3:20

Kaiden looked at the time on his phone and saw that it was already noon.

"I guess she's going to be a baby that allows us to rest at night," Kaiden chuckled. "At 3:20, we gotta put on 'Uncut Double X L'," Kaiden spoke. "Cool J has a surprise for us."

"I wonder what that could be," Samantha spoke as she raised the head of the bed to nurse Kailyn.

"I don't know, man," Kaiden chuckled.

He texted Ari, Byron, and The Prophet to let them know that the song was going to air.

Samantha's flash illuminated twice and she checked her phone.

Christina replied to her text with heart-eyed emojis.

Christina: 😍 😍 😍
Christina: she's sooooo pretty

Samantha smiled at Christina's text.

Samantha: thanks :)

Samantha placed her phone down and the nurses entered the room.

The lead nurse opened the curtains before speaking.

"I see you all are finally up," she chuckled. "How'd you all sleep?"

"She slept really well," Kaiden spoke. "She only woke up one time for food. Once Samantha finishes feeding her, I'm going to change her diaper."

"So she's going to be an easy baby," the nurse chuckled. "I wish mine was an easy child, but that's a different story. Good news is, we'll probably let her go home tomorrow if everything sits fine."

"Excellent news," Samantha assured her.

"I don't want to disrupt her from eating," the nurse added, "so once you all are finished changing her, ring for me to come in. I'll weigh her and all of that good stuff."

"Sounds excellent," Kaiden spoke as he rose to his feet.

***

"Samantha and Kaiden had their baby," Christina spoke as she ran her hands through Trequan's dreadlocks.

"Oh, word?" he asked. "Let me see her."

Christina showed him the picture that Samantha sent to her.

"She's going to be one spoiled baby," Trequan added with a laugh. "They're already cuddling with her."

"That's gonna be their issue," Christina laughed. "But she's so cute."

"She is. Congratulations to them. What's her name?"

"Let me ask Sam."

Christina texted Samantha and seemed to immediately get a reply.

Christina: what's her name?
Samantha: Kailyn Harmony Green

"Kailyn Harmony Green. I guess they decided to name her after her father."

"And peep the middle name. She's her daddy's daughter," Trequan spoke.

Christina's mind wandered off as to envision what it would have been like to be the one that gave birth to Kaiden's child, instead of Samantha. Her thoughts were interrupted by a text from Samantha.

Samantha: Kaiden has a surprise for me... I'm assuming it's a song. The surprise is at 3:20 our time, 1:20 your time on Uncut Double X L.
Christina: okay, I'll check it out

Trequan sat up.

"Tina, I want to ask you a serious question."

Christina always hated when that was stated; she knew it would lead to a conversation she didn't want to have.

She released a sigh before speaking.

"What's up?"

"What's the deal between you and Kaiden?" Trequan looked her in the eyes.

"What do you mean?" Christina defended. "Kaiden's just an ex that's dating my best friend."

"Seems to me like it's more than that."

"What do you mean?" she asked.

"I mean," Trequan rose to his feet, "I'm not stupid. I've seen how you are around him. You look like you're damn near ready to jump into his arms and kiss him."

"It's not even like that," Christina spoke as she pulled her pillow closer to her. "We were together for nearly three years and his bond with Isaias is unbelievable."

"So, you're really going to use Isaias to justify how you act around Kaiden?"

"I don't act a certain way around him," Christina spoke.

Trequan knew this wasn't going to go anywhere. Christina's ego was too large for her to admit her wrongs

"Fuck it," Trequan walked into the kitchen.

"No, we're going to talk about this," Christina rose to her feet and followed him into the kitchen.

Trequan opened the refrigerator and pulled out the Kool-Aid. He poured himself a glass and Christina continued.

"Give me an example of what makes you think I have a thing for Kaiden."

"Christina, you really don't want to do this right now," Trequan spoke. "Excuse me," he stated as he walked past her.

"No, answer me," Christina followed him into the living room.

"Okay, I'll entertain you," Trequan spoke. "Remember the concert a few months back? Man, when he got down on one knee, it seemed as though your heart sunk. Same for when he gave you a hug when we met up with them. And let's not forget the fight that went down. I didn't wanna get involved with that shit because I can't afford for them to *try* to pin something else on me, but you seemed like you wanted to kill ol' girl for talking shit about Kaiden. And then the hug before we all got in the car. If I wasn't there, I think you would have tried to kiss that fool."

"What the fuck?" Christina spoke, although she knew that some of the things that Trequan stated were true. "You just seeing stuff," she rolled her eyes.

"I told you to let the shit go," Trequan spoke, "because your ass can't admit to the truth when it's evident."

Christina fell silent as Trequan sat on the couch.

"You wanna know the truth?" Christina asked.

"It's whatever," Trequan spoke as he took a sip of his drink.

"Kaiden showed me something that no man has shown me before. It's because of him that I'm able to show love to you, Tre," Christina sighed. "So no, I don't have a thing for Kaiden. But because of that, and the fact that he and Isaias bond so tightly, it may seem like I have an emotional link to him."

Trequan didn't reply.

Christina sat down on the couch beside him and laid her head down on his chest.

"And that's the truth," she spoke.

"Well, at least you finally told me something," he answered.

Christina looked up and kissed him.

"I'm sorry," she uttered.

Trequan couldn't see himself being mad at Christina for too long. She didn't lie to him at all during their relationship, and he couldn't see himself letting it go over this.

Trequan kissed Christina and put his arm around her.

"You lie again and it's gonna be a problem," he stated with a chuckle although he was serious.

Christina didn't reply. She pulled out her phone and looked at the time and noticed it was 1:15.

"Oh shit," she quickly got up and walked to the room.

"What's wrong?" Trequan asked.

"Samantha wanted for me to tune into Uncut Double X L. She said there was a surprise coming up at 1:20 my time."

"You know what the station is?" Trequan asked.

"Satellite 294," Christina spoke as she turned to the channel on her computer's app.

"Welcome back to Uncut Double X L. I am your host Cool J. Check it out: I've just received this newest joint directly from your boy Kai G. It's by his artist Ari Love and it's featuring him. I've got the world premiere for you right here; this one is called 'Kailyn'. Take a listen and let me know what you think."

Cool J went off the air and played the track.

Christina and Trequan both listened to the track and were amazed.

"This is tight," Trequan spoke as he heard Kaiden come into the track.

"We know it's about his daughter and Samantha," Christina added.

Trequan continued to listen to the track and it got so silent, besides the rap, that you could hear a pin drop in the room.

"Cause, now you have my seed
It makes me want to cry
We still have to name her
'Kailyn is perfect', let's ride."

"That shit was cold, to be honest," Trequan spoke. "I never really gave Kaiden a listen until just now." Trequan finished his Kool-aid.

"Welcome back to Uncut Double X L. That was the latest from Ari Love featuring Kai G. Yea man, I just received word that my boy Kai G also just delivered a healthy baby girl. So big-ups to him and his family. Don't go anywhere, we got that new Cole on the way right behind this new one from Yachty."

13

"You know Isaias has been asking about you," Christina spoke over the phone.

"We're going to have to get the little guy out here to see me," Kaiden chuckled. "I miss seeing his face. Plus, he can meet Kailyn."

"How is she doing?" Christina asked inquisitively.

"She's doing well. Just celebrated her four-month birthday. She's such a happy baby," Kaiden spoke as he held Kailyn in his arms. "And every time she sees Ari or Smoove, her face lights up. She knows that means that there's going to be music made and played."

"She's truly her father's child. A music connoisseur."

"Her mama told me that she would always kick and move when I was in the studio."

"I believe that," Christina spoke. "How's Sam?" she asked.

"She's well. She went out with some friends so I agreed to take the night off to bond with my princess."

"Fucking with you, she's probably spoiled rotten."

Kaiden couldn't help but laugh.

"She's spoiled. But she's sweet and adorable."

Christina rolled her eyes as she walked into the washroom.

"Anyway, how are Trequan and Isaias?"

"They're both doing well," Christina responded.

She plugged in the curling iron so that she could do her hair.

"Tre is out with his boys and Isaias is with his grandma, so I'm about to find something to get into tonight."

"Well, me and Kailyn will be going to the studio and have her record a few vocals." Kaiden kissed the baby.

"Sounds like everyone's booked," Christina chuckled.

She was interrupted by a knock at her door.

"Kai, hold on. Someone's at the door," Christina set the phone down.

Christina left the washroom and walked to the door.

"Who is it?" she asked in a sing-song voice.

The person covered the peephole so that she couldn't look through it and see who it was.

"I'm not opening this door unless I know who it is," Christina stated.

The person didn't reply and Christina walked back to the washroom.

As she picked up her phone again, the person knocked at the door again.

Christina groaned with disgust.

"Whoever this is is about to piss me off," Christina replied into the phone.

Kaiden chuckled.

"Should I let you go?"

"Nah, it's good. Just hold on," Christina placed her phone in her back pocket.

She placed the chain-lock on the door and opened it.

"May I help—," she was stunned to see who was at the door.

"Hey, Christina," Brandon spoke.

She was speechless. She couldn't decide whether she wanted to close the door in his face or speak to him.

"You just gonna stand there?" he asked. "You're not going to invite me in or speak to me?"

"Now, why in the hell would I let you in?" Christina asked.

"Baby, I—."

"Let's correct that right now. I'm not your baby, I'm not your friend, I'm not anything to you," Christina replied.

"Nothing but my baby mama," he uttered.

Christina never told Brandon the truth about Isaias, so all this time, he thought that Isaias was his son.

Kaiden heard Brandon speaking, yet he'd never heard his voice before so he wasn't sure who it was.

Once Kaiden heard 'baby mama', he'd assumed it was Jordan.

"Christina," Kaiden called through the phone.

"Girl, now let me in to see my son," Brandon rattled the door.

"Brandon, go away. Don't make me call the cops."

"Girl, you can't keep me away from my son," Brandon replied.

"Goodbye, Brandon," Christina spoke as she closed the door.

"Tina!" he shouted.

Christina pulled her phone from her back pocket.

"Hello?"

"You good?" Kaiden asked her.

"Yeah... that was Brandon," she replied.

"Brandon?" Kaiden questioned. "How the hell did he find you?"

"I don't know," Christina answered.

"Do you think you should call the police?" Kaiden asked her.

"Nah, that fool isn't about to do anything," Christina assured him. "When he realizes that I'm not coming back to the door, he'll leave."

"I don't like the thought of him knowing where you live," Kaiden confessed.

"Don't even stress over it," she assured him as she returned to the washroom.

Kailyn played with Kaiden's chain that he wore around his neck.

Brandon knocked at the door again.

"Oh my, God," Christina groaned. "Go away, Brandon," Christina shouted.

"I'm not going anywhere until you talk to me," he replied through the door.

"You haven't told him that Isaias isn't his son?" Kaiden asked.

"No. When we moved away, I lost all contact with him," Christina confessed to Kaiden.

"You gotta tell him," Kaiden spoke. "It's only right." Kaiden looked at Kailyn. "I could only imagine how I would react if Kailyn wasn't my child and Samantha ran off and never told me."

"Then how about you tell him?" Christina chuckled.

"That ain't my business," Kaiden replied. "That's between you and Brandon."

"I knew you would say that," Christina shook her head.

"If you want, I'll stay on the phone in case something goes down once you tell him, but I will not tell him."

Christina liked the idea. Although no one would be at the house with her, at least Kaiden could alert Trequan and the authorities if something were to happen.

Christina walked to the door; her heart was beating fast and her hands were shaky.

"Hold on," she whispered to Kaiden.

She reached the door and made sure the chain lock was on the door. She opened the door slightly and spoke.

"Brandon, you may as well leave. Isaias isn't even here."

"Where is he?" Brandon asked.

"He's not here," she repeated.

"Tina, look. I'm sorry for how I was in the past. You and Isaias mean the world to me and I know I fucked that up. But I want to be in my son's life."

"Well, you better go have another child with someone else," Christina spoke.

"What?" Brandon asked.

Christina sighed.

"Brandon... Isaias isn't your son."

Christina could see the fury slowly start to fill Brandon's body.

"What do you mean?" he asked.

"While we were dating, you got abusive, and I needed comfort. I fucked someone else."

Brandon didn't reply. He turned his body away from Christina.

"Sorry," she whispered.

Brandon quickly turned around and punched the door.

The action startled Christina and she emitted a quick scream.

"Christina!" Kaiden shouted into the phone.

"Open this door, Tina," Brandon asserted as he tugged at the doorknob.

Christina grabbed ahold of the knob. She didn't want Brandon to potentially get in the house; she knew that if he did, it wouldn't end well for her.

She tried to pull the door shut, but Brandon's strength overpowered her easily.

"Open this fucking door," Brandon pulled at the door.

Christina feared that the chain lock would break as she tried to keep the door closed.

Kaiden heard the commotion and texted Trequan to let him know what was going on.

Christina didn't know how much longer she could hold the door closed.

"I go through all this fucking trouble of trying to find you and reconnect with you and my son, and you do this shit. You probably got another nigga in there right now, huh?"

"Brandon, we are not together," Christina replied. "Whatever I'm doing doesn't concern you."

"You right," Brandon stopped tugging at the door. "Aight, bet." Brandon walked away from the door.

Christina ensured both locks were on the door and fell to the floor; tears fell from her eyes.

She removed her phone from her pocket.

"Christina," Kaiden called out.

"It's okay. He's gone," Christina spoke although she couldn't stop the tears from falling.

"Trequan is on his way home," Kaiden spoke.

He felt really bad for Christina. She'd put herself in the situation, but he felt really bad for her. She'd trapped herself in the situation and although it happened in her past, it was catching up to her.

"I shouldn't have told him. Not right now, anyway. Some stories are better left untold," she cried.

"Yeah, but we have to tell them anyway. It's hard, I know, but things'll get better," Kaiden assured her.

Kailyn began to get fussy and didn't seem to want to settle down with Kaiden on the phone.

"Christina..." he started.

"I already know," she wiped her face with the nearby towel and chuckled. "Go on and take care of the little one. It's kind of funny," she sniffled.

"What is?" Kaiden asked.

"Now, I can say 'the little one' to you. You always say it to me," she giggled.

"You are a mess," Kaiden joked. Kailyn began to cry and Kaiden continued. "I'll talk to you later. Text me when Trequan gets there and if something pops off, don't hesitate to call me back," Kaiden defended.

"I will. Talk to you later."

"Bye," Kaiden replied as he ended the call.

He gently bounced Kailyn.

"Baby girl, what's wrong with you?" Kaiden asked her. "You wanna go make some music?" he asked.

She continued to cry as Kaiden walked down into the studio.

"Your mommy left us all alone tonight, so I need for you to be a big girl," Kaiden spoke as he sat in the chair, sat Kailyn on the table, and turned on the television. He turned to a baby cartoon to try to capture Kailyn's interest. It worked, but not that well.

"I know what'll cheer you up," Kaiden spoke aloud as he pressed play on his computer.

A mellow hip-hop instrumental played over the speakers and Kailyn's crying subsided almost instantly.

"Truly your daddy's daughter," Kaiden spoke to Kailyn as she smiled and reached for the mixer. "You already trying to learn how to work the board? Let's give it a few more months," Kaiden smiled as he picked her up from off the desk.

"Should I get in the studio?" Kaiden asked Kailyn as if he was expecting a response.

Kailyn reached for the mixer once again.

Kaiden kissed her on the cheek and moved her to his lap.

The two sat in the studio listening to different instrumentals until they both fell asleep.

Samantha entered the studio hours later and saw the two asleep.

"Kaiden," she whispered.

Kaiden slowly woke up.

"Hey baby," he repositioned the sleeping Kailyn and stood up. He kissed Samantha.

"How was it?" he asked.

"I had fun," Samantha spoke. "I had to get back to you and Kailyn. I knew you were probably struggling, which I can see you were," Samantha chuckled.

"Woman please," Kaiden laughed. "Funny story: she was being fussy, so I came down so she could watch cartoons. Kailyn didn't want to do that, so we played music instead."

"She is truly your child," Samantha said. She reached for the infant and Kaiden passed her over. "Did she eat?"

"Not since earlier. Maybe an hour before she went to sleep," Kaiden looked at the time. "That was about four-to-five hours ago."

"Let's go upstairs, Mama," Samantha spoke to Kailyn, who was still sleeping. "You coming, Daddy?" Samantha chuckled as she started up the stairs.

"You don't have to tell me twice," Kaiden joked as he turned off the lights and followed Samantha up the stairs.

Samantha laid Kailyn down in her crib before entering their room.

"Kaiden, can you undo this hook for me?" she asked about the fastener on her dress.

Kaiden walked behind Samantha and unfastened her dress.

"You know your girl is in some deep shit," Kaiden stated.

"Who, Tina?" Samantha asked.

"Yeah," Kaiden replied as she handed him her jewelry.

Samantha sighed.

"What has she gotten into this time?"

"Brandon showed up at her house earlier when we were on the phone. And she let him know that Isaias wasn't his son."

"Ooooh," Samantha spoke in disbelief. "And I know Brandon, so I know he wasn't thrilled to find that out."

"From what I heard, he tried to break down the door and kill her," Kaiden shook his head as Samantha slid down her dress, revealing only her lingerie.

"I gotta text her and make sure she's all good," Samantha walked over and sat on the bed.

Kaiden crawled into the bed behind Samantha and began to massage her neck.

Samantha moaned lightly but was determined to get her text to Christina.

"Tre messaged me earlier and let me know he made it to the house and that she was fine. They're probably resting," Kaiden kissed her neck as he maneuvered to position himself in front of her.

Samantha hated when Kaiden kissed her soft spot when she was trying to do something. He knew exactly how to make her weak in the knees.

"Baby, let me send this message," she struggled to speak.

Samantha: Tina, you okay?

She managed to press the send button before Kaiden kissed her neck again, causing her to lay back in the bed.

Kaiden gently bit Samantha's neck and she could feel waterworks.

"You don't know what you're doing right now," Samantha whispered with a chuckle.

"One word, two syllables," Kaiden started. "Kailyn," he laughed as he worked his way south.

Christina kissed Trequan before looking at her phone. She saw Samantha's text.

Samantha: Tina, you okay?

Christina figured that Kaiden must have told her what happened. She replied to the text.

Christina: Yea, I'm fine.

She wrapped Trequan's arms tighter around her as she reminisced on the day's events.

"Tre, I love you," she gently spoke.

"I love you, too," he responded as he kissed her on the cheek.

The sounds of the television filled the room before another word was spoken.

"You never told me about Brandon," he spoke.

Christina was silent.

"Tell me what I'm up against and if I should be worried," Trequan chuckled.

Christina knew that she had to tell him, especially since Brandon discovered where she lived.

"Brandon is an ex of mine. I was messing with him at the same time I was messing with Jordan, and so he thought Isaias was his son. Brandon was extremely abusive, so one day, my mom walked in on his episode, and she kicked him out. We moved away and I lost all contact with him."

Christina kept her head down.

Trequan didn't know what to say. He knew Christina had done some things in the past but didn't know the extent of it.

He kept his arms around her.

"Well, you don't have to worry. I'm here for you."

"I'm just scared at this point," Christina spoke. "You should have seen him when he came here."

"Yea, I saw the dent in the door," Trequan chuckled. "But we're going to get through this. If we have to, we'll even get a restraining order."

"Trust me," Christina slightly shook her head, "that won't stop him."

"Well if that doesn't work, he can always get these hands," Trequan tried to make her smile.

She adjusted in his arms and closed her eyes. For some reason, an image of Kaiden holding her appeared in her head.

"Did you tell your mother?" Trequan asked, interrupting her thoughts; she was glad he did.

"No, not yet. I don't want to drag her into my mess."

"She's already in it," Trequan replied. "If homie found out where you live, the next spot is to find out where your mama stays. He's on a mission to find Isaias."

Christina knew Trequan was right.

"Tre," she spoke.

"I'm just telling you the truth," he replied.

Christina sat up in bed.

"Now, go on and call her. And if she doesn't answer, send her a text."

Christina picked up her phone and dialed her mother's phone number. With each ring, Christina's heartbeat raced as she feared the worst.

The call went to voicemail and Christina hung up. She composed a text message and sent it to her mother.

Christina: Mom, answer the phone. I have to warn you about Brandon.

Christina sat her phone down.

"We've got to head over there," Christina replied. "She didn't answer."

"Don't trip over it," Trequan spoke as he looked at the time. It is 2 in the morning," he chuckled. "She could be sleep or doing the nasty," he chuckled as he buried his face in her neck.

"Why do you play so much?" Christina laughed.

"Just trying to make you smile," Trequan smiled.

"I love you," Christina spoke as she turned to face him in the bed.

"I love you, too," Trequan kissed her forehead.

***

"Brandon came by yesterday," Christina spoke to Sandra.

"Isaias' father, Brandon?" Sandra asked for clarification.

Sandra was under the impression that Brandon was his father; she didn't know that Jordan was the real father.

"Yes," Christina replied as she helped her mother fold the laundry. "I'm trying to figure out how he got my address," Christina set the shirt down.

Trequan was in the backroom playing with Isaias and Gary was at the gun range.

"Well, don't look at me," Sandra spoke as she put her dress on a hanger. "I haven't had any interaction with him since I saw him put his hands on you."

Sandra took a sip of her water before continuing with the next piece of clothing.

"What'd he want?"

"To talk to me and see Isaias. But I didn't have any words for him; what could we possibly have to talk about?" Christina chuckled. "But, he didn't leave until he got violent."

Sandra released a sigh.

"Tina, you let him in the house?"

"No," Christina immediately replied. "I kept the chain lock on the door, but it still didn't stop him from punching a dent in the door and nearly breaking the chain."

"But, why?" Sandra asked.

Christina knew the question was coming.

"I told him the truth," she spoke in a lower tone.

She hated that she'd be so dishonest with everyone. Since her past was catching up with her, she had no choice but to be honest; which was hard after lying for over five-and-a-half years.

"About what?" Sandra asked as she folded the shirt.

"Isaias… and the fact that he isn't Isaias' father."

Christina never looked away from the piece of clothing in her hand.

Sandra put the shirt down and looked at her.

"What do you mean he's not his father? Don't tell me that you don't know who the father is." Sandra spoke sternly, as this news upset her.

"Of course I know the father," Christina spoke. "I'm not a hoe," Christina continued to fold the shirt. "I just made a hoe decision," she chuckled.

"This isn't funny," Sandra replied. "Who's Isaias' father?"

"You're right, it isn't funny. But I gotta make light of the situation considering my life is on the line right now."

"Who's the father?" Sandra asked again.

Since Christina dated Kaiden, her respect for her mother increased tremendously. Whether she wanted to admit it or not, he had a strong effect on her personality. Normally, she would tell her mother to 'mind her fucking business', but since she dated Kaiden, she rarely cursed at her mother. She'd curse around her because that's who Christina was, but it was very rare that she'd find herself cursing to attack her mother.

"Jordan," Christina spoke.

"Oh, Tina," Sandra sighed.

"'Oh, Tina', what?" Christina asked. "You asked, so I told you."

"I'm just saying how that puts you in a bind. But you know, I can't stress over something that I can't change. Tell me exactly what happened when Brandon came over," Sandra powered off the television and had Christina place the clothing down.

Christina told her mother the details of when Brandon arrived, and she shivered as she discussed him.

"Did you tell him that Isaias was with me?" Sandra asked.

"No," Christina spoke. "I didn't tell him anything. But there's no guarantee that he doesn't figure it out; he found out where I lived."

Sandra shook her head.

"Well, hopefully, he just decides to leave."

"I don't know," Christina spoke, shyly. "He seemed pretty determined."

"Well," Sandra chuckled, "Gary has his gun card... let him come if he wants to," she laughed.

Christina chuckled at her mom.

"Speaking of fathers," Christina stated, "did you know that Isaias calls Kaiden 'daddy'?"

"He's smart," Sandra picked up another shirt. "He knows who would be the best choice."

Christina laughed.

"You know he has a daughter now."

"Yeah, with Sam, right?" she asked.

"Yes," Christina smiled. "Her name is Kailyn."

"Named after her daddy, I see," Sandra finished the final shirt.

"And guess what her middle name is."

"What is it?"

"Harmony," Christina laughed.

"Really?" Sandra chuckled.

"Yes! She's so cute," Christina pulled up a picture of the infant on her phone and showed her mother.

"Aww, look at her with her little microphone. Look at all that hair," Sandra laughed at the picture.

"She's her father's child, no doubt."

14

Kaiden entered the empty arena with Ari, Byron, and the security guards and police officers they'd hired. They all reached the agreement that due to their rapidly growing fame, they needed to invest in security; not to prevent them from talking to fans, but to protect their lives if something dangerous were to occur.

"This is what I'm talking about," Kaiden replied as they approached the stage. "Picture it," he spoke to Ari and Byron.

Ari looked around and saw the large arena; it was much larger than her first performance.

"This arena can fit a crowd of 200 thousand," the manager stated as he walked with them.

"Imagine selling out," Byron added, "and you know that we can do it."

"No doubt," Kaiden spoke as he envisioned selling out the stadium.

Everyone reached the front and Kaiden stepped onto the stage. He faced the direction of the imaginary crowd.

He thought about how it would feel to perform to a large crowd. It would surpass any performance he'd ever done.

"And the money would be A-1," Byron added.

"Shit, to be honest with you," Kaiden started, "I'm not even that concerned with the money. I mean, I am, but... here, come stand where I'm standing and look out," he replied. "You too, Ari."

Byron and Ari both came on stage and faced the 'crowd'.

"At King Pin, you know we're all about pushing the barrier and pleasing our fans. Just close your eyes and picture a crowd of 200k; screaming our names."

Byron and Ari both closed their eyes.

"What about the sound quality?" Kaiden asked the manager. "How will it sound with a sold-out arena?"

"The arena is designed to keep the noise in, yet let a little out into the outside world," the manager tried to explain.

Kaiden looked at him inquisitively.

"It's hard to explain," he admitted. "It's just something that you have to experience. We have some equipment in our storage area if you'd like to try it out."

"We gotta pay for that?" Byron asked as he opened his eyes.

"No, buddy," the manager answered. "It's on me."

They all left the arena through the back entrance and went backstage.

"Remind me to text Eddy and thank him for setting this walkthrough up," Kaiden spoke aloud.

"Okay. Remind me to remind you to text Eddy," Byron joked.

"You're full of it," Kaiden laughed.

"Think of it like this," the manager spoke again. "The arena is designed to keep enough echo in, but to release sound so that the sound isn't overlapping and bouncing off of each other."

"Oh okay, that makes more sense," Kaiden replied as they walked to the storage room.

"You all can store your equipment here leading up to the performance, if you choose to book the arena for your show."

"We'll keep everything on the tour bus," Kaiden replied as he considered it.

"Are you sure?" the manager asked.

"Positive."

The manager showed them the storage room and the layout of the entire arena so that Kaiden knew exactly what it was that he would be paying for and there weren't any surprises.

"What do you all think?" he asked when they reached the front.

"Well, it's got more than enough space," Kaiden admitted. "What do you all think?" Kaiden asked Ari and Byron.

"Kai, if it's good for you, you know I'm rockin' with it," Byron replied.

"When do you all want to throw this event?" the manager asked.

"7 months. Which is cutting it close, I know," Kaiden replied. "That's why when we leave here today, we want to be certain about the move we're going to make."

"Well," the manager took off his cap. "Let me leave you all for a moment to think about it. When you're set, come on over to my office."

The manager shook hands with everyone and walked away.

"So honestly, what do you all think? Can we pull this off?" Kaiden asked.

"We get out, bust our asses, and promote. If we get the audience, the rest is easy," Byron spoke.

"He's got a point," Ari added. "I mean, once we have the audience set, we're good to go. And it has to go beyond our regular means of getting the word out. We need more giveaways, promotions, appearances, and performances," Ari cleared her throat, "that is if we want to sell out."

"If we're not going to sell out, why are we even thinking of doing this?" Kaiden asked sarcastically. "You all know we aim high and we reach those goals."

"Work hard, play hard," Byron took a piece of gum from his pocket.

Kaiden and Ari both held out their hands simultaneously and laughed.

"Can't have nothing around black people," Byron chuckled as he gave them each a piece.

"If yall think it's worthwhile, I'll go write a check for the deposit right now," Kaiden spoke.

"Do that shit," Byron spoke. "You know we got your back and we're gonna go ham."

"Respect, bro," Kaiden spoke as they walked towards the manager's office.

The security guards took the lead as Kaiden pulled out his phone to text Ethan.

He and Ethan still hung out, but with both of their careers quickly taking off, they didn't have nearly as much time to hang out as they would have liked.

Kaiden: This venue is nice. The only thing is that it can sustain a very large audience so I gotta start promotion like, yesterday

Ethan: Word? Well you know I'm going to be there. Just lemme know what's up

Kaiden returned his phone to his pocket.

"We're going to book it," Kaiden spoke.

"Excellent," the manager replied.

He wheeled his office chair over to a file drawer and pulled out a folder.

"I just need for you to fill out this form to reserve the space, and there's a small deposit you have to put down."

Kaiden reviewed some of the questions on the application as Byron spoke.

"How small are we talking?"

"3500, if that's manageable," the manager answered.

"35?" Kaiden asked as he looked up from the form. "When my guy Eddy called up here, he was told it would be a two-thousand-dollar deposit."

"Who did he speak to?" he asked.

"He spoke to the manager, which is you."

He tried to remember speaking to someone and quoting them a price of two thousand.

"Yeah, think long and hard," Kaiden replied.

"Put it like this, dawg," Byron interjected. "We can give you this 2k now and you collect the rest later, or we can give you nothing and you take another buyer."

"Better ask about me," Kaiden spoke. "I'm legitimate."

"2000 now, and the other 8 on the day of the event."

"Sounds good," Kaiden shook his hand as he passed Ari the folder,

"These are just basic forms," she said as she shuffled through the papers. "Confidentiality, liability, security deposit, expectations."

"Take those home," the manager replied. "Bring them back later."

Kaiden wrote out a check for $2000 and handed it to the manager.

After their brief goodbyes, Kaiden, Byron, Ari, and their security guards all left the building.

"Okay, so now we're in this shit," Kaiden spoke as they reached the van. "We need to start pushing now and get our audience together. I'll handle getting together a lineup that people will be in high demand to see; maybe get Trey Songz or someone to accompany you, Ari. It'll make the girls and guys go crazy."

Ari chuckled before speaking.

"Guys?"

"Hell yeah," Kaiden laughed. "The guys are going to be all over you when they see you sing and perform with your sexiness," Kaiden chuckled.

Byron and Ari both laughed.

"Yeah, okay," Ari replied.

"No, but seriously," Byron said as his laughter subsided, "we're thinking of radio promotions, interviews, television appearances," Byron spoke.

"Everything," Kaiden reiterated.

Kaiden gave Samantha a call since he hadn't spoken to her since he left the house earlier.

"Hello?" she answered.

"My bride. How are you?" Kaiden asked.

"Just sitting here with *your* daughter," Samantha chuckled.

Kaiden could hear Kailyn crying in the background.

"So, now she's *my* daughter?" Kaiden joked.

"Whenever she wants to be a diva, she's all yours," Samantha laughed.

"You so silly," Kaiden spoke. "So, we just booked the venue, and now we're going to start pushing heavy to get the crowd we need."

"That's what's up. What's the capacity of the space?"

"200k," Kaiden spoke with excitement.

"That's your largest venue yet, isn't it?" Samantha spoke as she gently bounced Kailyn. She prepared her a bottle as Kaiden spoke.

"It will be. Hopefully my largest crowd. So I'm gonna need your help in pushing this, baby," he replied.

"You know I got you," Samantha replied. "But I'm going to tell you this," she spoke.

"What's that?" Kaiden asked.

"You need to get back here and get your spoiled diva, like yesterday," Samantha chuckled as Kailyn cried.

She wouldn't take the bottle and wouldn't seem to settle down.

"Put me on speaker," Kaiden emitted a little laugh while shaking his head.

"Go on," Samantha placed her phone on speaker so that Kailyn could hear.

"Little girl," Kaiden spoke.

Kailyn continued to cry.

"Kailyn," Kaiden sang.

Kailyn's crying subsided to whimpers.

"Why are we crying, baby girl?" Kaiden asked her.

Kailyn began to coo and make noises into the phone.

"I don't know why your mama is bugging," he spoke. "Acting like she can't stop you from crying."

"You know what," Samantha interrupted, "you are something else," she spoke to Kailyn and kissed her cheek.

Kaiden laughed aloud.

"I'm on my way home. Take her into the studio and play one of my tracks for her. She always has fun reaching for the board and talking into the microphone," Kaiden replied.

"Okay, baby. I'll see you soon. I love you," Samantha replied.

"I love you, too," Kaiden spoke as he hung up the phone.

Byron and Ari both laughed as he hung up.

"You are truly a family man," Byron spoke.

"It's all good, Smoove," Ari spoke. "He's a great father and that's all that matters," she chuckled.

"Yall are both some haters," Kaiden laughed.

"So, I guess we're about to go crash at your place," Byron replied.

"Negative," Kaiden replied. "You're about to take your ass somewhere and promote. I mean, you're not a family man," Kaiden laughed.

Byron rolled his eyes.

"Yeah, man, whatever."

"I'm just messing with you. You and Ari know you all are always welcomed in my home," Kaiden added.

"That's love," Byron spoke.

15

Christina and Isaias finished getting dressed for the concert.

Kaiden had originally sent her three VIP tickets, but Trequan couldn't make it this time around, so she and Isaias came alone.

"You ready to go see Kaiden?" she asked Isaias.

"Yes!" he spoke excitedly.

"You're gonna be my date for the night?" Christina asked as Isaias walked towards the door.

She turned off the lights and closed the door to her hotel room.

"I could be if you want me to," Isaias replied.

"That's my boy," she replied.

The two of them got on the elevator and Isaias talked about how he and Kaiden were going to hang out.

"And, we're going to hang out all night. Maybe we'll win another lion," Isaias spoke excitedly.

"You think anything's going to be open, baby?" Christina asked.

"It's always open with Kaiden," he replied. "And then I'm going to play with Kailyn and..."

"Take a breather, baby," she chuckled to get Isaias to stop talking.

The two of them walked out of the hotel and climbed into the Lyft car that Kaiden ordered to pick them up.

She knew that this wasn't like the charity event that was rated PG, but she wanted Isaias to be able to see Kaiden and get a chance to hang with him. She also knew this would be a perfect opportunity for him to meet Kailyn.

"You all ready for the concert?" the driver asked.

"Yes. I'm going to see Kaiden," Isaias blurted.

The driver chuckled.

"Yeah, well that makes one of us, little man. I wanted to go, but it was sold out before I even had the chance," he admitted.

"I guess it's good that we got these VIP tickets," Christina spoke as she took selfies on her phone.

"I know you paid an arm and a leg for those tickets."

"Nah, not even," Christina admitted.

"Kaiden gave them to us," Isaias blurted.

"Oh, yall got it like that?" the driver asked. "What made him give you tickets? Did you all win them or something?"

Christina sighed. This driver was asking a lot of questions and she truly didn't feel like having the conversation at the time.

"He's my ex," she spoke moments later.

"Oh," the driver replied. There was nothing more he could say than that.

The driver continued the drive in silence.

Christina (to Kaiden): We're almost there
Kaiden: Come in on the south wing. Samantha and Kailyn
are downstairs waiting for you.

"Guys, I have to make a slight detour. There's a car that's been trailing us since we left the hotel. California license plates."

Christina looked back and saw the car.

"Maybe they're going to the same place," she suggested.

The driver chuckled.

"Baby, I can tell you're not from here. This is Chicago and if you feel like someone's following you, you detour."

The driver turned right and the car turned behind him.

He made a few turns and the driver stayed behind him.

The Lyft driver pulled over to see if the driver that was following him would follow suit.

The car drove past.

"Still think he was following you?" Christina chuckled. "Now, take me to the arena."

The driver cleared his throat and continued the drive to the arena.

Upon arriving, she and Isaias saw Samantha standing and holding Kailyn.

"Samantha!" Christina called as she embraced her friend. Kailyn had her pacifier in her mouth.

"Hey, Tina," Samantha replied.

"How have you been?" Christina asked her friend. "It's been months! And this little one must be Kailyn."

Kailyn slowly blinked her eyes twice at Christina before looking at Isaias.

"Well damn," Christina chuckled. "Did I do something to offend?"

Samantha laughed.

"Don't mind her. She's just daddy's little diva," Samantha ran her fingers through Kailyn's hair.

Kailyn tried to move Samantha's hand and Samantha wasn't the least bit surprised.

"Oooh," Christina spoke. "She truly is a diva."

"I told you," Samantha chuckled as she kissed Kailyn. "Can you believe this little one is already trying to walk?"

"As her father's child, yes, I can believe it."

Isaias extended his hand towards Kailyn. He'd never seen a baby up close like this, so it was kind of exciting to him.

"She's mean, Isaias," Christina joked.

"She's a baby, Mommy," Isaias joked.

Kailyn reached over and grabbed ahold of Isaias' finger. She used her free hand and took her pacifier out of her mouth and held it. She tried to put Isaias' finger in her mouth.

Christina and Samantha both couldn't help but laugh at how adorable this was.

Christina gently pulled Isaias' finger away and Samantha feared that Kailyn would cry at this.

"You shouldn't have done that, Tina," Samantha chuckled.

Kailyn returned her pacifier to her mouth and sat up in her mother's arms.

Christina gave Samantha a look.

"Oh, so if I'd have done it, you would be crying," Samantha spoke to Kailyn.

"She's a trip," Christina spoke again. "Where's Kaiden? Isaias wants to see him. You know that's all he's been talking about." Christina looked down at Isaias. "Mommy, where's Kaiden? When are we going to hang out? We're gonna spend the whole day together,'" she mimicked her son.

Samantha let out a small laugh and shook her head.

"He's somewhere running around with Ari and Byron; trying to ensure this is all set-up as it should be. I'll call him," she replied.

Samantha called Kaiden but could barely hear him when he answered.

"Yeah, baby, where are you?" she shouted.

"I'm upstairs in that second conference room that we saw. What's up?" he replied.

It wasn't nearly as loud where Kaiden was.

"Isaias is looking for you," she replied.

"Okay, go to the suite that I reserved and I'll be over in about five minutes," Kaiden spoke.

Samantha hung up her phone and walked over to the suite with Christina and Isaias.

"Kaiden's giving you all the VIP treatment," Samantha chuckled. "Personal security outside of your room. You're still close enough to the crowd yet you're separate... you got it good," she chuckled.

"Yeah, yeah. He just needs to get his ass down here and not keep my baby waiting," Christina held Isaias' hand tightly.

"He should be here shortly," Samantha replied as she sat down.

Christina sat in the chair next to Samantha and Isaias sat next to Christina. He wheeled his chair over to be close to Kailyn.

"Kaiden's thinking of debuting his daughter to the crowd," Samantha stated.

"That should be exciting," Christina chuckled. "I know it's going to cause the crowd to go crazy."

"Yeah, but I'm not sure how I feel about that. I mean, it's already hard enough to keep our lives personal, and the fact that he literally had to hire security to keep us all safe, doesn't stop my mind from wondering about all the crazy people out there. For example," Samantha adjusted Kailyn in her arms, "what if Jada or her boyfriend try to hurt Kailyn?" Samantha worried.

"As crazy as I think Jada is," Christina touched Samantha's arm, "I don't think she would even try something that bold," Christina remembered the fight from earlier. "She talks of good game, but I can tell she isn't about that life."

Christina and Samantha looked at Kailyn as she made noises at Isaias as if she were having a conversation with him.

Samantha put her hand in Kailyn's hair and adjusted her ribbon.

"Mommy, she's not mean," Isaias giggled. "She's just cute." Samantha smiled.

"You friends with her already, Isaias?" Samantha asked as she removed her hand from Kailyn's hair and put it in Isaias' hair.

"She's fun," he replied.

Before another word was spoken, Jada entered the room.

"Speak of the devil," Christina spoke.

"Hey," Jada spoke in a low tone.

Samantha held Kailyn tighter.

"You come back to start some more shit?" Christina asked. "Don't think that because we're in this public place that I won't give you round two."

Samantha was praying that nothing occurred in the room with Kailyn there.

"I didn't come here to cause trouble," Jada spoke as Damian entered and the security guards closed the door. "I was out of line," Jada spoke.

"That's for goddamn sure," Christina spoke in a low tone.

"I was hurt, traumatized, and I am—," Jada cleared her throat, "*was* in love with Kaiden."

Christina held Isaias' hand.

"I shouldn't have attacked you, physically," she looked at Christina and Isaias, "your son, verbally. Or you, mentally and emotionally," she spoke to Samantha.

Christina and Samantha didn't say a word.

"I'd like to apologize as well," Damian stepped forward. "What happened wasn't right, and shouldn't have happened," he smiled. "I just hope that you can forgive us for what happened."

"And why should we do that?" Samantha asked. "I mean, yea, you apologized, but what's that necessarily mean?"

"Precisely what we just said," Jada spoke. "What we did was wrong. We just wanted to offer you an apology. Whether you accept it or not, is on you. Either way, we'll be out of your hair and gone for good."

Jada looked at Kailyn and Samantha held her tighter.

"That's Kaiden's little girl, isn't it?" Jada chuckled.

Samantha didn't reply.

"I'm not going to try anything. At one point, I didn't feel like I had an exit..." Jada scratched her ear. "But now, I'm exploring different avenues. I'm free."

Isaias stayed beside his mother. The previous incident with Jada rang in his mind and he feared another fight may occur.

"Come on, D. Let's get out of here and back to our seats," Jada turned around and headed out of the door with Damian.

A few moments after she left, Christina spoke.

"It took everything in my power to stop me from choking that bitch. She had the audacity to come here and try to apologize after she said what she said and did what she did."

"Well, I'm glad you didn't," Samantha spoke. "This could have gone badly for everyone. You, Isaias, me, Kailyn, the crowd, Kaiden's artists, and even Kaiden," she continued to stroke Kailyn's hair.

"Well, it's over with," Christina spoke. "I'm grateful for that," she looked at Isaias, "and you should be, too."

Samantha kissed Kailyn on the cheek as Kaiden walked into the room.

"There they are," he spoke as he wiped his face with a towel.

"Uh-huh," Samantha spoke. "Your hoe just left," Samantha rolled her eyes as Kaiden approached her.

Kailyn's eyes widened as she saw her father and reached her arms for him.

"Who?" he asked as he sat down and took Kailyn.

"Jada," Christina answered.

Isaias ran over to Kaiden and hugged him.

"Kaiden!" he shouted.

"Hey, buddy," Kaiden replied as he returned the hug.

"She came in here on some apology shit," Samantha finished. "To hell with that."

"Oh," Christina replied as she swallowed her sip of water, "her man came as well."

"What the absolute hell?" Kaiden replied. "If they come back, make sure you all give me a call. I'm going to have to see why security let them in," he shook his head.

"Kaiden, are we going to hang out after the concert?" Isaias asked.

Kaiden played with Isaias' hair with his free hand.

"Yeah, little man. Me, you, and Kailyn are gonna play together after this is over."

Kailyn continued to suck on her pacifier and looked at Isaias.

Christina felt a bit of relief. She hadn't heard Isaias call Kaiden his father in a long time.

"You like ice cream?" Kaiden asked Isaias.

"Yeah!" Isaias squealed.

"Okay. Me, you, and Kailyn are going to get some ice cream after the show," Kaiden looked at his watch. "But right now, I gotta get out there. I just wanted to come by and see you before I went on stage."

Kaiden kissed Kailyn on the cheek, gave her back to Samantha, and fist-bumped with Isaias.

He kissed Samantha on the lips and gave Christina a quick hug.

She still liked the way it felt when Kaiden hugged her. Although she was dating Trequan and Kaiden was engaged to Samantha, Christina couldn't help but feel a small spark when they touched.

Little did she know, Kaiden didn't like to connect with her because he felt the same spark that she did. But he didn't want to go back to that; he knew he wasn't going back. Samantha and Kailyn were his life, and he'd do whatever he had to do to prove it to them.

But he couldn't help but hug Christina. He hugged her to be polite, but at the same time, he felt as though it gave him a 'push' to do his best.

"Sam, don't forget about what I told you for the last track," he spoke as he walked to the door.

Samantha rose to her feet.

"I won't," she called out. "Go on and kill them," she encouraged.

Kaiden turned around and walked close to Samantha.

He gave her a passionate kiss so that they were body-to-body. Christina felt a little awkward with this occurring.

Christina covered Isaias' eyes.

"You trying to give Kailyn a sibling, huh?" Samantha whispered as their lips were centimeters apart.

"Nope," Kaiden chuckled, "you just inspire me, baby."

Kaiden turned away and exited the room and jogged to the stairs to go backstage.

"Everyone set?" Kaiden asked over his earpiece.

"Let's do it, boss," Byron spoke.

"Kill the lights. I'm walking onto the platform now," Kaiden spoke as he walked onto the platform that would lift him onto the stage. "It's showtime," he replied.

The lights to the stage went off and the crowd started to cheer.

DJ Hitman played a suspenseful instrumental and the smoke machines began to emit a ton of smoke onto the stage.

The platform started to slowly rise and the pyrotechnics shot flames from their spots.

Christina, Samantha, Isaias, and Kailyn all watched from their suite.

"Holy shit," Christina spoke.

Although the show was just starting, she knew it was going to be good from the introduction.

The instrumental grew greater in dynamics and the bass dropped as Kaiden reached the top of the stage.

The strobe lights started to flash on Kaiden and he spoke over the microphone.

"Ladies and gentlemen, did you all come here for a show?" he spoke.

The audience cheered louder.

"I can't hear you, I said 'sold out muthafuckin' Bark Arena, did you come to see a muthafuckin' show'?"

The audience cheered louder and Kaiden felt the vibrations.

"That's what the hell I'm talking about," he spoke as he walked closer to DJ Hitman.

"Make some noise one time for my A1 since Day 1 DJ," Kaiden spoke as the spotlight shone upon DJ Hitman.

The audience cheered loudly and he continued to play the instrumental at a comfortable volume so that Kaiden could comfortably speak.

"Got the lovely 'Soul Ladies' singing in the background," Kaiden spoke as the light shined down upon the four ladies. "And let's not forget the geniuses you will see tonight, including hit artists Ari Love, B. Smoove, and Lester the Prophet!"

The audience cheered loudly and Kaiden chuckled.

"Ladies and gentlemen, allow me a moment to introduce myself for those of you who may not know me. I am your boy Kai G and I'm just a small-town hero," he chuckled and the audience laughed and cheered. "I come from where you're from: Chicago, city of dreams."

Kaiden continued as the audience cheered.

"Since I'm a local, I know about the struggle. I know how hard it is for someone to get their big break. So later in the show, and I hope you singers and rappers got your raffle tickets; later in the show, we're gonna bring three of you all on stage to perform one song apiece. If it's hot, I'm gonna sign you," Kaiden replied.

The audience seemed to go crazy at Kaiden's announcement.

"Now, since we're doing big things and progressing in life, me and King Pin have decided to appropriately name this 'No Turning Back'."

Kaiden picked up his water bottle and continued to pace the floor as the audience cheered.

"Reason is, like I said, we're moving forward. Just like in life, you can't press 'reset' when you don't like the way things are going. If you fail a test, unless you got a cool ass teacher," Kaiden laughed with the audience, "you can't go back to that shit. Once it's done, it's done. Us putting on this show for you, we're locked in this shit, we can't go back and undo it. But here's the thing, we're trapped doing what we love for who we love. We sold you the tickets and promised to give you a good time; there's no turning back from any of that," Kaiden shrugged his shoulders as the audience cheered.

"So remember that shit with life. You can't take back the choices that you make. What's done is done. You either accept it and grow from it, or you let it eat you."

Although he wasn't throwing any kind of subliminal messages to anyone, Christina and Samantha both felt the message that he was portraying.

He was right. Things happened in their past, and they happened for a reason. If they were to sit around and consistently bring it up, they would never move forward.

"So, with that being said," Kaiden shouted. "I'm Kai G, and I hope you all enjoy what we're about to present to you," Kaiden spoke as he walked off stage and the lights to the stage went off.

There was complete silence and utter darkness for a second. Kaiden left the audience stunned. They weren't sure of why the stage went dark, but since there was no audio or visual for at least 30 seconds, they quickly became disappointed.

"Boo," an audience member shouted and the rest of them joined in.

"This is bullshit," another member yelled.

The pyrotechnics shot flames into the sky as dancers ran onto the stage and the lights rose again.

The crowd cheered as Lester ran on stage.

"One time for my boy Kai G," he shouted.

The audience cheered as he continued.

"Ain't no technical difficulties, *bih*; we just had to make sure that you all weren't sleep," he laughed. "But let's do this shit right," Lester spoke. "Hitman, hit that shit."

***

"You all have been wonderful tonight," Kaiden replied. "Bryson Tiller and C-Sharp both came out here with Ari and they absolutely killed it. But before we close this show out, I want to bring Ari out here to help perform this last track."

The audience cheered loudly as Ari walked back onto the stage.

"I know you all are familiar with the track 'Kailyn'."

Ari embraced Kaiden and stood beside him.

"That track was written by this beautiful young lady right here," Kaiden motioned to Ari and the audience cheered louder.

"Now, I have one request of you all," Kaiden spoke loudly. "Ari's going to sing acoustic, so I need for this crowd to silence the cheers. And while she's doing this, we're gonna make this bitch dark, alright? So the only lights I want to see are the flashes and lights from those phones."

The audience members began to quiet each other.

"Ladies and gentlemen, Ari Love," Kaiden gave her another hug and walked backstage as the stage lights completely went dark.

The only light that was present was the spotlight that shined down on Ari.

The band members began to play the instrumental to *Kailyn* and Ari started to sing.

While backstage, Kaiden called Samantha.

"Baby, you ready?" he asked.

"Getting set-up now," she mentioned.

"Perfect," Kaiden spoke.

He pressed a button on his earpiece and spoke.

"Make sure Samantha isn't seen and is brought around through 'gateway D'."

He looked at his watch before proceeding to walk back to the stage.

The instrumental peaked as Ari concluded singing and Kaiden walked onto the stage rapping softly into the microphone.

The crowd went wild as the second spotlight followed Kaiden as he came onto the stage.

"I knew you were mine
The moment I saw those eyes
Shining brighter than anything,
Just let me visualize
The touch of your skin, your soul, your hair
It is all so smooth
This is the last thing in the world
That I'm willing to lose."

The audience began to rap alongside Kaiden and he paused as he looked out into the sold-out arena. The only lights that were on were the flashes of the phones.

A tear formed in his eye as he realized the amazing product he'd just produced.

Kaiden joined in and picked up on the rap while Ari vocalized.

"I have no problem
If you need the space
I'll sit myself down
And set my own pace
We can do it slow, baby
Who said it's a race?
You are my medicine
Shit,"* he chuckled, *"you know I want a taste*
When I fall asleep at night
That's when I dream of us
I combust, not a moment in the day that I fuss
Cuz' I know I have you & until the track busts
Our train will continue together we must..."
"She's coming up now," Kaiden heard over his earpiece.
He slowed the tempo of his rap down.
"Cause, now you have my seed
A sight that makes me want to cry."
Kailyn started to coo and make baby noises into the microphone as Samantha rose to the stage.

A third spotlight turned on and shined on Samantha and Kailyn.

The pyrotechnics shot fire into the air.

"We still have to name her," Samantha stated in a soft, melodic manner.

Once the audience heard Samantha's voice, the quiet cheers quickly erupt into erroneous screams. This was something that no one expected.

Kaiden took a pause and the spotlight followed him as he walked over to Samantha.

He gave her a passionate kiss and the audience cheered so loudly that the entire stage vibrated.

Kailyn reached for her father and Kaiden took her into his arms.

He held Samantha's hand and walked back to his previous position on the stage.

Ari couldn't help but shed tears and tried to control it, but her voice cracked as well. Christina applauded as the two kissed and cried tears of joy as Isaias looked on and smiled.

Kaiden looked into the crowd and continued with the final line of the rap.

"Kailyn is perfect, let's ride."

Flames shot from the pyrotechnics and Kaiden adjusted Kailyn on his arm.

She looked into the crowd and made noises into the microphone.

The drummer banged on the cymbals to build the announcement.

"Kailyn Green," Kaiden shouted into the microphone as the spotlight shined on her.

The audience cheered loudly and Kailyn giggled.

Kaiden pulled her down and kissed Kailyn on the cheek.

"Yall have been wonderful," he announced as Byron, C-Sharp, and Lester came onstage.

Ari joined them and stood beside Kaiden.

"This has been a King Pin production. I'll see yall next time," Kaiden spoke as he turned away with Samantha.

Samantha, Kaiden, and Kailyn all walked off the stage and into the walkway of the arena.

The audience continued to cheer loudly as DJ Hitman mixed for the outro.

Byron, Ari, and C-Sharp waved to the crowd and walked offstage, leaving the audience cheering for an encore.

Christina left the suite and walked downstairs to the arena floor to go backstage with her passes.

Security let her backstage and she saw Kaiden.

Isaias smiled and ran up to Kaiden.

Christina wiped the tears that accumulated in her eyes from the event.

"That was wonderful," she spoke to Kaiden and Samantha as they held hands.

Kaiden hugged Isaias with his free arm.

"It's all because of this man," Samantha chuckled as she kissed Kaiden on the cheek.

"I love you," Kaiden uttered.

"I love you, too," Samantha replied.

Isaias tugged at Kaiden's sleeve.

"Kaiden, are we still going out for ice cream?" he asked.

"Yea, man," Kaiden answered. "Let me finish a few things here and we'll go."

16

It took Kaiden an hour-and-a-half to finish things up before he was ready to go. He had to go over the next move with his artists, finalize some numbers with the manager, and finish things related to the performance.

He also took a moment to meet a few fans that may have run into him.

He took ahold of Isaias' hand and held Kailyn into his arms.

"Me and Tina are about to use the washroom really quickly," Samantha spoke. "We'll see you outside."

"I'm going to need for you all not to take all day," Kaiden chuckled. "Kailyn, Isaias, and I will be waiting."

He gave Samantha a quick kiss.

"Yeah, yeah," Samantha replied with a chuckle. She and Christina walked into the bathroom.

Kaiden walked outside of the arena with Isaias walking on his right side. He held Kailyn on his left side.

"And I want to get a triple scoop of chocolate," Isaias spoke as the security guards escorted them to the car.

Hundreds, if not thousands, of fans were still at the arena in the parking lot; all hoping to get a chance to meet Kaiden and his daughter.

"You want all of that, huh?" Kaiden chuckled as fans surrounded him.

"Stay behind me, Mr. Green," the security guard spoke as he walked them to the car.

"Form a perimeter around Mr. Green," Kaiden heard the guards say as they repositioned themselves so that they formed a pentagon and Kaiden, Isaias, and Kailyn were in the center.

Christina and Samantha walked outside and saw the security escorting Kaiden, Kailyn, and Isaias to the car.

Christina looked to her right and saw a vehicle with the headlights off.

It didn't take long for her to notice that this was the same vehicle that was trailing her while she was in the Lyft car.

"You see them?" Samantha asked with a smile.

Christina heard Samantha, but at the same time, she didn't. She was too focused on the vehicle.

She could see someone in the vehicle looking in the direction of Kaiden.

The person put their dreadlocks into a rubber band and put on some glasses.

"Girl, are you listening to me?" Samantha chuckled.

Christina tapped Samantha.

"Look over there… in the red Subaru," Christina spoke.

Samantha looked over at the vehicle.

"What about it?" Samantha asked.

"That car was following the Lyft driver earlier. And I can't make out who it is."

Samantha gave a good look at the driver and her heart skipped a beat as she saw a reflective object in the car.

The driver exited the vehicle and Christina saw that it was Brandon.

She realized that he must have been keeping his eye on her and following her ever since she told him that Isaias wasn't his child.

"Oh, shit, it's Brandon," Christina panicked as he walked towards Kaiden.

Samantha quickly reacted.

"Kaiden!" she shouted as she and Christina ran down the stairs.

Brandon stepped closer to the guards, but was still about thirty feet away. He pulled out a pistol with a shiny grip.

He aimed the gun through the small spacing of the perimeter set forth by the security. The barrel was aimed directly at Isaias.

It caused him great pain to learn that Isaias wasn't his, especially the way he found out.

Kaiden heard his name called and looked to his right. He saw the gun aimed.

He made a slight movement from the perimeter set forth by the security guards and jerked Isaias, pulling him behind him.

At the same time that Kaiden pulled Isaias, Brandon shot the weapon.

The crowd started screaming and running to their vehicles.

The bullet entered Kaiden's hip as he winced in pain and fell to his knees.

"Daddy!" Isaias screamed to Kaiden as he ran to the right side of Kaiden.

The security guards responded after the first shot, pulled out their weapons, and aimed. The five security guards remained around Kaiden and never broke formation.

Brandon saw Kaiden holding a baby and felt a little bad that he hit Kaiden, but then he heard Isaias call Kaiden his father.

The anger he was feeling took over his body and he fired the weapon four more times. He was determined to kill Kaiden, Kailyn, and Isaias.

Kaiden managed to lay Kailyn on the ground and shielded both Kailyn and Isaias by positioning his body over them.

Brandon's second bullet hit Kaiden in his arm. The remaining bullets entered Kaiden's right rib, his right thigh, and the final shot hit Isaias in his left calf.

Isaias screamed in pain as Kaiden shielded him.

The security guards shot Brandon multiple times and killed him as a result.

Once he was down and the gun flew from his hand, a security guard ran over to Brandon with his gun aimed.

He put his fingers to Brandon's neck to ensure there wasn't a pulse.

Christina and Samantha reached the security guards and Samantha fell to her knees and cried. Samantha turned Kaiden over on his back and saw that Kailyn and Isaias were both crying.

Kailyn wasn't hit by any bullets; Kaiden shielded her completely.

There was blood in Kaiden's mouth as he looked at Samantha.

"Baby, get up," Samantha cried as she picked up Kailyn.

Christina picked up Isaias and held her hand over his wound.

Tears fell from her eyes as she held Isaias and looked at Kaiden.

"Baby," Samantha cried as she rocked back and forth with Kailyn.

Kailyn wailed loudly as Samantha cried.

"Boss, come on," one of the security guards spoke.

Kaiden gasped for air as he struggled to breathe.

"Baby, you need to stay with me," Samantha rocked Kailyn in one hand and held Kaiden's head up with the other. "Has anyone called a fucking ambulance?" she shouted.

Byron and Ari were the two artists who were still at the arena and came running outside once they heard the commotion.

"Kaiden!" Byron shouted as he held Ari's hand.

They ran down the stairs without any security surrounding them.

"All these fucking people standing around," Samantha shouted at the bystanders, "call for fucking help!"

"Sam, they're on the way," the security guard spoke.

"They're not coming fast enough," Samantha shouted. "Get him in the car and take him yourselves," she spoke frantically.

"Sam, listen. We can't do that. If we move him, he could lose blood at a faster rate."

Byron and Ari reached the crowd and Byron quickly removed his jacket.

He got on his knees and put the jacket over Kaiden's rib to try to stop the bleeding.

"Don't you fucking leave, Kai," Byron held back his tears.

Ari couldn't hold her tears back.

"Breathe, bro," Byron pleaded.

Kaiden fought to keep breathing and keep his eyes open, but with every breath he took, it felt as though his lungs were collapsing and more blood shot into his mouth.

Kaiden squeezed Samantha's hand.

"I love you," he managed to whisper.

As Kaiden fought for his life, his life flashed before his eyes and thoughts ran through his mind.

God, I can't go right now. I have a fiancé who needs me. I have to look after my daughter and protect her. My family... What about my family? How will they move forward without me? Paralyze me, make it so that I can't physically perform. Do what you want, but don't take me. I'm not ready to go. Lord, please. Can I live?

Samantha felt the squeeze and looked down at him.

Her tears fell onto his face.

"Baby, stay with me," she rocked back and forth.

"Samantha, give me Kailyn," Ari spoke. "She doesn't need to see this," Ari held her composure although the tears flowed from her eyes.

Samantha didn't listen as she was crying to Kaiden.

Ari reached down and got Kailyn from her mother's arms.

"Fucking hell, man," Byron spoke.

Sirens sounded as ambulances and police vehicles turned into the arena.

A team of paramedics quickly unloaded from the vehicle and took the gurney from the back of the vehicle.

The first person they ran to was Kaiden.

The teams bent down to Kaiden; Byron slowly lifted Samantha off the ground.

"Come on, Sam, we have to let them do their jobs."

She didn't want to release Kaiden's hand but she knew that she had to let him go so the paramedics could work on him.

One paramedic removed his shirt and looked at the bullet entries while another put an oxygen mask on him.

"Let's get him up," they spoke as they lifted Kaiden and put him on the gurney.

They loaded the gurney into the ambulance and the second set of paramedics loaded Isaias into another.

Samantha cried on Byron as Ari held Kailyn.

"Where are you all taking him?" a security guard asked the paramedics as they were loading into the ambulance to drive off.

"We're taking him to Rush," the paramedic replied.

"I'm going with him," Samantha spoke loudly.

Samantha reached to Ari, and Ari passed her Kailyn.

The paramedic opened the back door and Samantha climbed inside with her daughter.

"Sam, we're gonna meet you there with the crew," Byron shouted.

The paramedic that was holding Kaiden drove away from the scene and Samantha took hold of Kaiden's hand again.

17

Samantha sat in the waiting room outside of the ER. She found herself sitting alongside Byron, Ari, C-Sharp, Kaiden's mother and grandparents, Ethan and Cody, and Kailyn.

Christina sat in the hospital room with Isaias. The doctors confirmed that the bullet just grazed his calf and caused a tear, so he would need a cast and crutches, but nothing life-threatening.

"Let's not put any negative energy into the air," Byron spoke aloud. "Kaiden needs us right now, and so we have to lift him up."

Samantha tried to think positively, but she was having a really hard time.

Kaiden meant the world to her, and she couldn't imagine losing him. It was more than her she was concerned about; what about little Kailyn?

Kailyn was asleep in Samantha's arms; Kaiden's blood covered her dress.

"Please God," Samantha spoke aloud.

Kaiden's mother pulled Samantha close and embraced her. This was another person that Samantha knew was hurting the most. Samantha kissed his mother on the cheek and cried on her shoulder.

"Shh," his mother whispered.

Samantha didn't understand what Kaiden could have done so wrong that Brandon targeted him, although, she knew that when Christina told her about him coming back around, it wasn't good news.

A doctor came out of the room and spoke.

"Kaiden Green?" he asked and everyone stood up.

"Doc, how is he?" Samantha asked, partially afraid of his answer.

"Mrs. Green," he assumed by looking at the ring on her finger.

Samantha didn't correct him.

"Your husband sustained multiple gunshot wounds. He took one to the hip, his leg, his arm, and his rib. The hip, leg, and arm wounds aren't the issue; it's the one to the rib."

"What do you mean?" Samantha's voice cracked as she held Kaiden's mother's hand.

The doctor continued.

"The bullet cracked his rib, which is an issue but not too major. What is major, however, is that the bullet continued and pierced his right lung, which has caused severe internal bleeding."

The tears fell down Samantha's face and his mother petted her.

"But he's going to make it, right?" Kaiden's mother asked.

"We've removed all of the bullets and have attempted to slow the bleeding by using a blood transfusion. His body has not yet responded to the transfusion."

"Just tell us the truth," Samantha spoke with her face buried into Kaiden's mother's shirt.

"We're doing the best that we can," the doctor spoke in a low tone. "Right now, he's connected to a breathing machine and we're seeing if his body responds to the transfusion."

"Please, do what you can," his mother spoke.

The doctor returned to the operating room.

"I think we should begin a prayer," his mother spoke.

Samantha looked at her and then around the room.

Many fans heard the news about what had happened and decided to come to the hospital for support.

"Kaiden needs all the support he can get," his mother continued, "let's lift him up."

Everyone who was in the waiting room for Kaiden gathered in a circle in the best way that they could.

"Heavenly Father, we are all kneeled today to ask that you provide your son with strength. Provide him with the strength needed to fight through this." She paused.

The tension and stress in the room were at their peak.

"We pray that you work through these doctors today. Give them the ability to help your son; this father, fiancé, friend, and manager to many. Please put healing hands on your child, and breathe life into the doctor's hands to help him pull through."

Samantha squeezed his mother's hand tighter as she started to cry.

"Please allow us to see his smile again. Allow us the chance to hear his voice and play with him again. In your name, we pray, amen."

Everyone opened their eyes and Samantha embraced Kaiden's mother and grandparents.

"I'm going to see if I can go back there with him while he's in the room," Samantha spoke. "He's on life support and I want to be at his side."

His parents agreed.

"Here, let me get Kailyn," Kaiden's grandmother spoke as she took the sleeping baby.

Samantha walked to the front desk and asked for permission to be at Kaiden's side. The nurse who came out was reluctant at first, considering Samantha was crying and she wanted to spare her emotions but agreed to let her back.

Samantha put on a sterile gown over her clothes and was escorted to the room.

Samantha saw Kaiden with an IV in his arm and stitches over where the bullets entered his body.

He was connected to the breathing machine with many monitors connected to him.

Samantha sat in the chair next to him and held his hand.

"Kaiden, I know you're hurting," she began, "but I need for you to be strong, baby," she sniffled.

He didn't respond in any way, although she didn't expect him to.

"If only you knew all the people that are in the waiting room," Samantha chuckled as she interlaced her fingers with his. "You got your fans out there, your mom, your grandparents," Samantha inhaled slowly. "Byron, Ari, C-Sharp, Ethan, and Cody."

Although Kaiden wasn't physically responsive, Samantha was positive that he could hear her and his spirit was present.

"We're all waiting for you to pull through so that we can see your smile and talk to you again, baby. Especially Kailyn. You know that's your little diva."

The heart monitor sounded in rhythm and Samantha looked at Kaiden.

He lay there wearing nothing but his underwear and the gown the staff put on him.

This wasn't the image she wanted of Kaiden; she kept hoping that he would wake up and speak to her.

She didn't say a word; she held his hand tighter.

She synchronized her breathing with the machine's. An article that she'd read in the past, exercised the idea that a couple who synchronized their breathing performed better on an emotional and spiritual level.

Although it wasn't necessarily him breathing, she felt it would be the same concept.

She rose to her feet and kissed him on the forehead.

"I love you," she whispered.

Samantha felt her phone vibrate and she pulled it out of her pocket.

Christina: What's going on?
Samantha: It's not looking good. The bullet penetrated his lung and now he's on a fucking machine

Christina felt sick to her stomach hearing this. To make matters worse, she felt that she was the cause of this. Because of her actions in the past, it was causing a chilling effect on her present and would have one against her future.

Samantha: how's Isaias?
Christina: Doc says he's gonna be fine. The bullet grazed his calf muscle but he'll be okay. He's gonna need crutches and wear a cast for a while.

The tears began to fall from Christina's eyes as she read about Kaiden.

"Why are you crying, Mommy?" Isaias asked as he laid in the hospital bed. "Is Kaiden okay?"

Christina thought about everything she'd done in her life but paid close attention to the things surrounding her and Kaiden. All the things that he'd ever done for her or told her were finally making sense; it was to better herself. Kaiden didn't mean any harm in any of the things he said and he meant every word.

She thought about how much Kaiden truly loved her and Isaias, and how his love for Isaias continued even after the breakup.

"Yes, baby. Kaiden is fine," Christina lied.

Christina: :(this can't be real

Samantha saw the text and placed her phone down.

"Kaiden, don't leave me," she pleaded. "Kailyn is going to need her father and I'm going to need my husband by my side."

Suddenly, the heart monitor's beeping increased.

Samantha turned her head and looked at the monitor as it said his heart-rate was increasing. It was at 135 beats-per-minute.

Seconds later, the heart-rate decreased back to its previous speed of 78 beats-per-minute.

Again, it increased to 120 before dropping seconds later.

"Kai, stop playing," Samantha cried as she laid her head on his chest.

Samantha began to reminisce on the memories of her and Kaiden.

Nurses ran into the room.

"What's going on?" Samantha asked.

"He's coding. Mam, we're going to have to ask you to step out of the room," one of the nurses hurried her out of the room.

"What does that mean?" Samantha frantically asked.

"Mam, we will let you know as soon as we get everything situated," the nurse rushed.

They closed the curtains and blinds as Samantha was forced out of the room.

Samantha (to Christina): he's coding.

Samantha walked through the doors to return to the waiting room.

18

"It's a sad day across America, as we have learned that Kaiden Green, also known by his rapper name, Kai G, has died after being shot, following the first stop of his 'No Turning Back' tour here in Chicago. Kaiden had just wrapped up his performance when he was shot and killed by Brandon Thompson: a 30-year-old male from Bakersfield, California. Thompson was killed immediately after shooting Green. Green was 24."

Christina slowly approached the casket as Sandra and Gary sat by Kaiden's parents. Isaias also sat with them, considering his leg caused him pain to stand for more than a few seconds.

Many celebrities attended the funeral; including Ari, Byron, DJ Hitman, Lester, The Phelonies, and C-Sharp.

If Kaiden hadn't been there – Christina didn't want to think about it; it was horrific to even consider. To be here at Kaiden's funeral, she wondered how she could even hold herself up.

Although she was dating Trequan and had grown to love him, and Isaias had grown accustomed to him, she knew that deep down, her feelings for Kaiden would *never* go away.

Christina soon found herself standing over Kaiden's lifeless body as he lied inside of the white casket.

"Hey, baby," Christina let out a tear as she whispered it to Kaiden as though he could hear her.

She placed her hand on his chest.

"I keep telling myself that I'll end up waking up from this nightmare, but this shit is real," she whispered.

Christina studied Kaiden's face and it almost seemed as though he were smirking at her.

"I keep waiting on that phone call or for someone to wake me up and say this is all a dream, but I know it's not going to happen. Not once did I ever expect to be at your funeral; not right now and not under these conditions," Christina began to let the tears flow and she spoke to Kaiden's body.

"I know it really doesn't mean much now," Christina continued. "But I truly am sorry for everything. If only I'd taken what you told me seriously, you'd probably still be here with me and Isaias... well, you'd be here with Samantha and Kailyn; me and Isaias would be in the background," she gently chuckled.

Christina tried her hardest to hold it together as the crowd watched her look at Kaiden's body for this extended period of time, yet no one dared to disturb her.

"I promise you, even though you're no longer here with me in the physical, I will not disappoint you... And don't worry about your daughter," she added, "I will do my best to help Samantha raise her and I will make sure she doesn't follow *my* path, but the path that *you* would like her to travel."

Christina reached in her pocket and pulled out folded pieces of paper.

She placed the papers in Kaiden's breast pocket of his suit.

"I know you can't physically read it," she chuckled yet cried, "but if your spirit ever has time, I wrote down what you wanted. I will live by it. I just wish I could have made this change a while ago. I know you would have made the ideal husband – you always were special."

The usher started to walk over to Christina.

"Baby, looks like I have to go now," Christina cried even harder. Her tears fell onto Kaiden's face. She leaned forward and kissed him on his cheek.

"I'm sorry," she spoke seconds later after retreating from the kiss.

Christina walked away and returned to her seat.

By now, she couldn't stop the tears from falling. She held Isaias tightly, who was now crying because his mother was crying.

"Good morning, everyone. Brothers, sisters, family, and friends of Kaiden Green. We are all gathered here to give our brother a proper homegoing." The pastor spoke as the ushers closed the casket.

"Another life lost too soon due to gun violence," he added. "An innocent soul at that. Kaiden was never involved in gangs, guns, or drugs... but since he is no longer here on this Earth, we know that the man upstairs is taking care of our brother now," the pastor gently spoke.

He looked over at Christina and continued.

"Now, I'd like to open this ceremony with a verse from the book of Roman, verse 14, line 7. It reads," he cleared his throat, "'For none of us lives to himself, and none of us dies to himself. For if we live, we live to the Lord, and if we die, we die to the Lord. So then, whether we live or whether we die, we are the Lord's. For to this end Christ died and lived again, that he might be Lord both of the dead and of the living.' Brothers and sisters, even though Kaiden is no longer here on Earth with us, we know he is with our Lord," he finished and the audience applauded.

"Preach on, Pastor," a lady shouted.

"Now, I would like to invite this young lady to the stand," he motioned to Christina.

She was in shock.

"Family, join me in welcoming her to the podium," he spoke as he started to applaud.

Christina felt as though her heart was about to stop. She wanted for Kaiden to be alive and there with her, not lifeless and in a casket. Although her mind was telling her not to move, it felt as though something, or someone, took control of her body and walked her up to the podium.

Christina looked at the crowd and seemed to freeze. She looked over at Samantha and saw her friend holding her baby tightly and crying hard.

Kaiden's death took a toll on Christina, but it had to hit Samantha even harder.

"Hi everyone," Christina spoke. "My name is Christina Parker. Kaiden and I dated for nearly three years before we decided to go our separate ways, but I would say we remained good friends... I honestly couldn't let him go," she looked at the casket. "I don't want to let him go now," the tears started to flow more heavily.

The preacher gave her a box of Kleenex.

Christina continued to speak.

"Kaiden was special. His mindset was so different from that of today's generation. He was one of those people where you knew you would have a good time if he was around."

Christina sniffled and made eye contact with Kaiden's mother. Tears flowed down her face.

"My heart really goes out to his fiancé and their child; my best friend, Samantha Williams. It's weird that my best friend is engaged to my ex and has his child, but I truly believe that brought us all closer together; call it crazy if you want."

Samantha couldn't stop the tears from rolling down her face and landing on the infant.

Samantha felt as though her whole world was crumbling down since Kaiden died.

"In fact, I want to bring Samantha up once to speak about Kaiden. She'd be in a better position to do so." Christina shifted her attention to his mother. "Mama Green," Christina continued over the mic. "I know we had our differences, but I want you to know that I am here for you if you need me. I can't even imagine the pain that you're going through right now. Kaiden was your world, and I know you never expected to be here today. We had many fights and arguments, but I do want for you to know that I love you," Christina was careful with her choice of words.

Kaiden's mother managed to rise to her feet and walk over to Christina. The two shared a long embrace.

The audience applauded as the two embraced and Samantha stood with the infant in her arms.

Samantha reached the podium and hugged Christina and Kaiden's mother.

Samantha adjusted the microphone and tried her hardest not to look at the casket. Christina and Kaiden's mother returned to their seats and held hands.

"I honestly don't want to believe this," Samantha spoke with tears in her eyes.

She rocked the infant gently.

"I don't have anything prepared, so you all have to bear with me. My eyes are heavy, my heart is heavy, and my mind is all scrambled. My whole world has crumbled to pieces since he passed."

Samantha looked into the audience and saw Christina holding Isaias tightly.

"Kaiden's a hero," Samantha continued. "All of his life accomplishments show this." The tears began to flow down her face, "Kaiden protected Kailyn and Christina's son, Isaias, from harm. But to do that, unfortunately, it cost him his own life."

For the first time since the original walk-in, Samantha looked at the casket.

"He can't go," she proclaimed as she cried harder.

Samantha felt her knees weaken as she started to lose her balance.

She turned away from the microphone and grabbed on to the casket.

"Kaiden, I love you," she shouted. "It may be selfish to want you back, but please come back to me."

At times like this, Samantha questioned her faith and belief in God. Samantha regained her composure as if she could feel Kaiden holding her up. Kailyn started to wake up.

"I know they say that God has a plan," Samantha spoke over the microphone, "but I really want to understand this plan."

Kailyn started gurgling and making baby noises, and Samantha gave her finger to the infant.

"My fiancé dedicated his entire life to ensuring that his daughter could have one," Samantha felt weak again.

Samantha grabbed a Kleenex from the box and wiped her eyes.

"But I do know one thing's for sure: Kaiden Green will always be watching over myself and his daughter."

The audience started applauding at Samantha's comments.

"Kaiden was one of a kind, and I know I'll never have true happiness since he's no longer with me. But I'll remain strong for him, for me," Samantha looked at Kailyn, who had the tip of Samantha's finger in her mouth, "for little Kailyn."

Kaiden's mother cried harder as Samantha spoke. She'd wished that things had gone differently and that she still had her son; not only for her sake but to be a husband to Samantha and a great father to his daughter.

"It kills me on the inside because I don't want to let you go, but I know it's time to do so. Kaiden, I love you so much, and I just want you to know that."

Samantha turned away from the podium with Kailyn.

"Can you all...?" she asked the ushers as she looked at the casket.

Two of them looked at one another and nodded before walking over to the casket.

"You sure?" one usher asked Samantha.

Samantha sharply inhaled.

"I'm ready," she spoke as she held Kailyn tighter.

The ushers opened the casket and revealed Kaiden's body.

She inched closer and touched Kaiden's chest.

"Sleep easy, baby."

Upon touching Kaiden, she couldn't stop the tears from falling from her eyes.

"I love you," she whispered.

She leaned forward and kissed him on the lips.

What she imagined would be cold and stiff, felt warm and tender, as though Kaiden's spirit was with her in that instance.

Samantha stood up straight after kissing Kaiden and allowed Kailyn to reach over.

Kailyn touched Kaiden's body and gurgled a sound that sounded like 'kay'. Samantha could have sworn Kailyn was trying to say her father's name, but all babies made random noises, so she wasn't in a position to swear by it.

Samantha returned to her seat as Ari approached the podium.

Kaiden's mother hugged her daughter-in-law and her grandchild as Ari spoke.

***

After the repast, Christina returned to Kaiden and Samantha's home.

"So, what are you going to do, girl?" Christina asked her.

"I'm going to stay here. I'm going to build on what Kaiden started; it's what he would want," Samantha sniffled as she looked over to Kailyn.

Christina looked at the infant asleep in her bassinet.

"She's so beautiful," Christina spoke. "She sleeps just like her daddy. Looks like him too," she chuckled as she held her friend's hand.

"That's why we named her Kailyn. Tina, I swear, whenever Kaiden was in the studio making music, Kailyn would just be kicking and moving around in my stomach like there was a party," Samantha smiled. "Yeah, she loves music just like her father."

Christina smiled as she looked over to Isaias, who was sitting on the couch holding the car that Kaiden had gotten him.

"Maybe, when she's older and ready, you can tell her the story of her father. Let her know about his legacy and how much he loved her."

"I'm not a songwriter," Sam chuckled. "I'll pitch the idea to Ari or Smoove. Let them work their magic. I'm sure he would prefer his story to be told through music."

Christina shrugged her shoulders.

"Kailyn needs to know that her daddy loved her with all that he could. Just make sure she understands that."

"I will," Samantha spoke. "Look," she exhaled, "I know I'm young, but I think I'm going to legally take on his last name. And I don't know if I want another."

Christina looked at her friend sternly. She could see that Samantha truly loved Kaiden, maybe even more than she did.

"Sam," she gently spoke, "taking on his last name is fine. But I don't think Kaiden would want for you to be lonely at his expense. Kaiden wants you to be happy and to keep living. He'll *always* be with you."

Samantha leaned in and embraced her friend as tears fell from her eyes.

"I love you, Tina," she cried softly.

"I love you too, Sam," Christina spoke.

Moments passed before another word was spoken.

"Girl, Isaias and I brought some extra clothes from the hotel. We're gonna go shower and get changed, and once we get out, we'll all go out and do something special," Christina spoke.

Samantha sighed.

"Okay," she spoke. "You know how to work the shower, right," she forced a chuckle.

"I wasn't born yesterday," Christina replied, jokingly. "Come on, Isaias."

Isaias stood up and walked over to Samantha. He gave her a long embrace.

Samantha smiled and hugged Isaias tightly, and followed the hug with a kiss on the cheek.

Christina rose to her feet and took Isaias' hand in hers; they walked to the bathroom.

Samantha lifted Kailyn from her bassinet.

Samantha returned to the couch while holding the infant.

She pulled her phone and went to her photos. She came across one of the videos that Kaiden recorded when she was in the hospital about to have Kailyn.

"Come on," Kaiden spoke over the video as he adjusted the camera to capture the two of them in the shot.

Samantha smiled but let tears flow as she saw Kaiden in such a happy state. She loved how she could see the sparkle in his eye as he looked at her, and when the two kissed in the video, her heart nearly skipped a beat.

"I love you," he spoke over the video.

Although he was speaking over the video, Samantha felt as though he were sitting next to her, whispering 'I love you' in her ear.

"I love you, too," Samantha spoke aloud.

She cried as she continued to watch the video.

"She'll be here soon, guys! I may record her birth."

Samantha laughed aloud.

"Baby, your father was a trip," she spoke to Kailyn.

Kailyn cooed at the video of the two.

Samantha continued to watch the video.

"They've already seen our sex tape," Samantha heard Kaiden's laugh both in the video but also in her ear; she could tell his spirit was present, watching over her and Kailyn.

The video started to shake wildly from Kaiden dodging the pillow she'd thrown at him.

"I'll talk to yall later," the recording ended and Samantha silently cried.

The next picture in Samantha's photo library was the picture of Kaiden and Kailyn sleep in the hospital chair. Samantha scrolled over to one more picture and came across the professional picture that she, Kaiden, and Kailyn had taken at the mall. There were hearts around the border and a big heart encompassing the three of them and a caption that read 'We're *Your* #RelationshipGoals'.

Christina turned on the shower and got undressed. She undressed Isaias and they both got into the shower.

As the warm water hit her body, she couldn't tell if tears were falling from her eyes or if the water was just making her face wet.

She looked down at Isaias and ran her fingers through his curly hair. She reminisced on all of the times that Isaias spent with Kaiden, and how the two had bonded.

Isaias looked up at his mother.

"Mom," he gently spoke.

"Yes, baby?" Christina asked him.

She wasn't sure what he could be getting ready to ask her or what he was about to say.

Whatever it was, she wasn't mentally prepared to handle whatever questions he could have had.

Isaias had an inquisitive mind, and since they'd just left a room with Kaiden laying down in what appeared to be a bed to Isaias, he was wondering why everyone was crying. He cried during the funeral because his mother was crying, but didn't quite understand why.

The two of them skipped the burial, as Christina knew Isaias wasn't ready to see that and she knew she'd break down in tears to see Kaiden's casket lower into the plot.

Christina couldn't imagine how Samantha got through the burial without managing to bring Kaiden's body back with her. She could only imagine the tears shed by Kaiden's fiancé at the burial ground.

Christina couldn't help but picture Samantha jumping on top of the casket as it lowered; she chuckled inside from the thought. That's how much Samantha loved Kaiden.

Isaias rubbed his eyes free of water before continuing. "When is Daddy coming back?"

Kaiden,

You asked me why I am the way I am.
Coming up, I had love; so, like, I knew what it was
with family, but wasn't too sure about it when it came to
~~boy guys~~ men. My mother had her issues and my
father was in jail; I was, basically, raised by my grandparents;
I'm sure you remember them; you know they paid you lol
It wasn't until I came back to my mom that I met
Brandon. But while we were dating he became abusive, and that's
when I met Jordan. I swear I wasn't this wild child
that everyone makes me out to be. I was on a search to
find *LOVE*; and call me weird, but I used sex as the
determining factor to ~~figure~~ out if I was loved, even though
I did tell you that sex wasn't important

That's why, when I met you and you didn't want to do anything with me, I was hurt. I felt like you didn't love me.

We had our issues ~~during our~~ relationship, ~~and when, Jordan~~ ~~got out,~~ even though we wanted to make things ~~right,~~ we were on a shaky path. I honestly still loved Jordan, so during our relationship, there were times that he was on my mind although I truly loved you. ~~He and I did~~ what we did and I can't take it back... and when I saw the hurt and pain in your eyes when you showed up and learned what you did, I knew at that moment that I'd lost you. Even though you ~~always~~ told me that if I ever messed around with him, we would be done, I just wanted a family and I ~~felt~~ felt that I could get that with Jordan – –

Once we broke up, I needed a sense of security. I knew I didn't pay you much attention or even attempt to fix it right away, like I should have, but since you were in a relationship and in love with Sadie, I decided to give things with Jaden a try. It wasn't until he got really abusive that I left (olga ~~and you~~ know). After ~~the~~ our relationship ~~with you~~, I compared all guys to you and held them to your standards, no one compared. But then I met Trequan. It started as a "hit and run" as your boy J. Cole would say b/. We honestly were just fuck-buddies, that's it, but when you and ~~I~~ reconnected, I stopped doing that with him, but I never stopped talking to him as a friend, kind of ~~like~~ like a rebound. And when I felt that you weren't giving me attention or the time-of-day

I went back to him.

I will NEVER forgive myself ~~all~~ for what happened. I broke your heart and did what I knew would hurt you, but Kaiden, the truth is, I love you. I've loved you ever since you first sent me flowers, and my love got deeper once you flew me out here, and I'm going to continue to love you until the day I die. Seeing you with Samantha made me cry on the inside & out, because I knew how she would treat you. I knew she would be a better ~~girl~~ girl to you than I was... and I knew you would end up proposing. But I can't change any of that, so it's no point in crying about it. I'm going to stand by Samantha as she ~~raises~~ raises Kailyn, and I will do right by them; I promise.

Kaiden, I love you and I will continue to love you until

the day I ~~didn't~~ die. I'm sorry I didn't let you
know any of this sooner. You were my *FIRST* true love,
but I ~~still~~ foolishly hurt you... and the moment I did
and saw the hurt in your eyes
that N I knew there was ~~to too~~ No Turning Back.

~~Chr~~ -Christina Parker ♡

* Love Always, Baby *

I Love You,
Xander

Kaiden,

You asked me why I am the way I am. Coming up, I had love; so, like, I knew what it was with family, but wasn't too sure about it when it came to me. My mother had her issues and my father was in jail. I was basically raised by my grandparents; I'm sure you remember them; you know they loved you lol. But it wasn't until I came back to my mom that I met Brandon. But while I was dating him and he became abusive, I met Jordan. I swear I wasn't this wild child everyone wants to make me out to be. I was on a search to find love; and call me weird, but I used sex as the determining factor to figure out if I was loved, even though I did tell you that sex wasn't important. That's why, when I met you, and didn't want to do anything with me, I was hurt. I felt like you didn't love me.

We had our issues during our relationship, I know, and when Jordan got out, even though we wanted to make things right, we were on a shaky path. I honestlty still loved Jordan, so during our relationship, there were times that he was on my mind although I truly loved you. He and I did what we did and I can't take it back… and when I saw the hurt and pain in your eyes when you showed up and learned all that you did, I knew at that moment, that I'd lost you. Even though you always told me that if I ever messed around with him, we would be done. I just wanted a family and felt I could get that with Jordan   -_-.

Once we broke up, I needed a sense of security. I know I didn't pay you much attention or even attempt to fix it right away as I should have, but since you were in a relationship and in love with Jada, I decided to give things with Jordan a try. It wasn't until he got really abusive that I left (déjà vu, I know). After our relationship, I compared all guys to your standards; no one compared. But then I met Trequan. It started out as a 'hit and run' as your boy J. Cole would say lol. We honestly were just fuck-buddies; that's it, but when you and I reconnected, I stopped doing that with him. But honestly, I never really stopped talking to him as a friend, kind of like a rebound. And when I felt that you weren't giving me attention or the time of day, I went back to him.

I will NEVER forgive myself for what happened. I broke your heart and did what I knew would hurt you, but Kaiden, the truth is, I love you. I've loved you ever since you first sent me flowers, and my love got deeper once you flew me out here, and I'm going to continue to love you until the day I die. Seeing you with Samantha made me cry inside because I knew how she would treat you. I knew she would be a better girl to you than I was… and I knew you would end up proposing. But, I can't change any of that, so it's no point in crying about it. I'm going to stand by her side as she raises Kailyn and I will do right by them; I promise.

Kaiden, I love you and I will continue to love you until the day I die. I'm sorry I didn't let you know any of this sooner. You were my first true love, but I foolishly hurt you… and the moment I did that and saw the hurt in your eyes, I knew that there was no turning back.

-Christina Parker

www.ingramcontent.com/pod-product-compliance
Lightning Source LLC
Chambersburg PA
CBHW030310200626
46816CB00002BA/840